The Two Fiddlers

George Mackay Brown lives and works in the Orkney Islands where he was born. He went to Newbattle Abbey College in Midlothian and later read English at Edinburgh University. He has never travelled farther south than Scotland.

Amongst the awards he has received as a writer are the Scottish Arts Council Literature Prize in 1969, the Katherine Mansfield Short Story Prize in 1971 and the OBE in 1974. *The Two Fiddlers* is his first book for young people.

Also by
George Mackay Brown in Piccolo
Pictures in the Cave

George Mackay Brown

The Two Fiddlers

Tales from Orkney

text illustrations by Ian MacInnes
cover illustrations by Paul Slater

Piccolo Pan Books

First published 1974 by Chatto & Windus Ltd
This edition published 1979 by Pan Books Ltd,
Cavaye Place, London SW10 9PG
© George Mackay Brown 1974
ISBN 0 330 25772 2
Set, printed and bound in Great Britain by
Cox & Wyman Ltd, London, Reading and Fakenham

to Anne

Contents

Introduction

Orkney, Edwin Muir the poet said, is a land where the lives of living people turn into legend. What he meant probably was that in a small community, enclosed by sea and sky and field, it is possible to see a man's life as a whole. It has a clear outline. It becomes elemental and larger than life.

The islanders have always loved legends. In previous generations, on a winter night there was nothing else for them to do but tell stories and play their fiddles.

They told stories, of course, about their neighbours, and about the laird and the minister and smugglers and lovers – the vivid people who were a part of their own circumstances.

Their imaginations were touched too by some of the strange phenomena around them. There were certain mysterious things that needed an explanation. What were the green mounds beside the road – the 'knowes' – that became so mysterious on a midsummer night? What were those immense tall stones that stood in the fields, and at Brodgar circled endlessly in a stone dance? Why were certain of the Hoy hills littered with scree?

Nowadays archaeology and science supply, in their cold fashion, many of the answers that the Orkneymen of old pondered with wonder and delight.

Still farther back the story-making art went, probing elemental things. What is the connection between music and corn and death? Why is the sea salt? What is the sky made of? Why do the seals love music more than the other animals? The enchanting tongues went on and on beside the fish-oil lamps. Then the grey of morning entered the crofts, and called the islanders back once more to their hard work of ploughing and fishing.

Scandinavians came to Orkney in the early centuries of

our era, first as Viking raiders, then as settlers and colonists. They dominated the native Pictish population. Until the islands became a part of Scotland 500 years ago, the language and art and law were exclusively Norse. The people told stories that were common all over the north of Europe, with here and there an intricate Celtic image or episode. As we get nearer to modern times, Scottish names become common.

Now, alas, the story-making gift is waning in the islands; and will wane increasingly as we watch our television serials on a winter evening, and read sordid ugly 'real' stories out of the newspapers.

The stories in this book are a few of the many that used to be told. Here and there I have let my imagination play upon certain bare or difficult patches, so that the young readers might find the whole more readable. I acknowledge the stimulation I have had from Mr Ernest W. Marwick's *An Anthology of Orkney Verse* and his *Creatures of Orkney Legend and their Norse Ancestry; The Orkney Saga*; and the folk-lore essays of the late Duncan J. Robertson in *The Orkney Book* and in *The Proceedings of the Orkney Antiquarian Society*.

George Mackay Brown

1 The two Fiddlers

Once there were two young men returning home late on a summer night. (In Orkney it is never dark at that time of year.) The two young men, whose names were Storm and Gavin, carried fiddles, because they had been all evening at a wedding, and they had been paid by the bride's father to make music for the dancing. Storm and Gavin, the fiddlers, were also rather drunk, because the wedding guests had plied them liberally with whisky and ale, to make the dance go better.

Now the young men were going home, rather unsteadily,

through the midsummer twilight. They spoke about the events of the evening, the bonny face of the bride, the parsimony of the bride's father, the unworthiness of the bridegroom to possess such comeliness, the good ale contributed by this farm, the sour ale from that croft, the clumsiness of the dancers, the marvellous cheese and oatcakes.

They were approaching a region that had an uncanny reputation, as the abode of ghosts and fairies and trows. In a field next to the road were two or three grass-covered mounds. Inside them, it was believed, the supernatural creatures dwelt.

The drink and the music had made Storm and Gavin reckless, but still they stepped warily and spoke in louder voices than usual as the cluster of knolls stood low against the sky in front of them, and blazed a vivid green in the twilight.

Neither wanted the other to know that he was a little afraid. They gripped their fiddles till their knuckles were white, and lurched on.

Gavin was telling Storm how he had taken a fancy to one of the wedding guests – a girl from the other end of the island. And he thought the girl liked him well enough too, for she had smiled at him from the floor of the barn more than once . . .

Gavin's voice fell on the midnight, unnaturally loud.

He went on to say that unfortunately there was no way of speaking to the girl. He had been paid a shilling to play the fiddle. The bride's parents would take a poor view of it if their hired fiddler deserted his music to pay compliments to one of the wedding guests; perhaps invite her out under the stars. There was nothing to be done about it. Gavin would like to know what Storm would do in such a situation . . .?

The knolls smouldered under the midnight sky like broken emerald.

When Gavin turned to Storm, the better to hear his answer, there was nobody there. Storm had disappeared.

'Well,' thought Gavin at first, 'he's fallen in a ditch. I didn't know he was as drunk as that. I've been wasting my breath. I'd better help him home, I suppose. His mother will give me a bit of breakfast for my trouble . . .'

But Storm was not lying in the ditch, though Gavin went back a hundred yards searching for him.

'How mean,' said Gavin to himself. 'He's very selfish, that Storm. He's gone off home by himself across the fields. I would never do a thing like that.'

(The truth is that Gavin was more than a little jealous of Storm. Storm had every kind of advantage over Gavin. He was handsome and graceful whereas Gavin was clumsy and coarse-featured. Also Storm was popular with the island girls and Gavin had no success with them at all; his story of the mutal attraction between a girl at the wedding and himself had been pure invention, meant to impress the other young breaker of hearts. But most important of all, Storm was a famous fiddler, well-known all over Orkney, whereas Gavin had never got much beyond the stage of scraping and ranting.)

'Well,' said Gavin to himself, turning his face homeward, 'I'll have a few words to say to him next time I see him. Some friend!'

From the heart of the knoll music flashed out: the unmistakable rhythms and cadences of Storm's fiddle.

Gavin shrieked with terror. He clutched his fiddle to him. He ran all the way home and fell panting through the door of his parents' croft. Later, when he thought about it, it amazed Gavin how he ever got home, for he had been in a trance of fear. Sometimes it seemed to him that his home-faring had lasted only a couple of seconds. And at other times the way seemed interminable; he had made the journey like a man of stone, with all the vengeful creatures of earth and air and water and fire after him in full cry.

Yet there he was next morning, lying on his bed at home, not a fiddler or a liar any more, but a poor crofter's son who had a hard day's work in front of him.

And as he lay and wondered, he heard a few old women going past the open croft door calling and lamenting, 'Storm Kolson's vanished! He never came home last night. O dear! He's drowned in the bog! He's gone over the cliff!'

What happened to Storm was this.

As he walked along the glimmering midnight road, listening to the empty brags and regrets of Gavin, a door swung open in the largest knoll and a voice said, 'Welcome, master. The folk inside are wanting to dance but they have no music. Honour us with your presence, man.'

Storm peered in at the door. At the end of the corridor he saw a magnificent hall hung with silks and woven tapestries. But the folk who stood here and there in groups were poor inert sick-looking creatures, with green rags hanging from them.

When the folk in the great chamber saw Storm standing in the door, they crowded about him eagerly. In particular they put looks of gratitude and joy on the fiddle. They fingered it delicately; they caressed it; one went so far as to pluck a string. Then they took Storm gently by the elbows and led him up to a man and a woman who were sitting on the high seats at the side of the hall.

'The music, lord, it is here,' they said. 'The young man has come of his own accord. He has brought the fiddle that sings so well.'

Storm had never experienced such courtesy as he got from these people.

The lord of the hall said to him, 'Young man, we are sorry to take you out of your way. We know that you have been fiddling all night at the wedding at Blinkbonny farm, and that you have work to do in the morning. But we would be very glad if you were to play one or two tunes for us. Then we will let you go.'

Storm answered that he would be glad to do that.

The lord ordered a steward to bring some refreshments to the musician. Storm was set down on an ivory-and-satin chair, and a golden cup brimming with wine was put into his hands, and a piece of bread tasting of honey was put into his mouth. He pledged his hosts and drank. The folk clapped their hands.

Then Storm stood up, put his fiddle under his chin, and began to play. The dance passed before his half-closed eyes, marvellous surges and eddies and chasms of green, like wind among young corn.

It was all over quite soon.

He stood on the dais with the silent quivering fiddle in his hand, and the score of dancers looked at him with flushed grateful faces.

'We thank you, musician,' said the lord. 'Your music has given us great joy. It has put new strength into us.'

The lady sitting beside him smiled at Storm; then leaned over and kissed him.

'Thank you,' said Storm. 'I don't know where I am, that's the truth. But my fiddle sounded better in this place than in any other place, and the dance was much statelier than that bunch of yokels blundering round and round at the Blink-bonny wedding.'

'It is the same dance,' said the lord. 'Before you go, Storm, we would like to grant you a favour; anything you wish.'

Storm was tongue-tied for a moment. He couldn't think of anything for himself. He already had everything that makes life pleasant – youth, and attractiveness, and talent, and a good appetite, and enough money from his father the merchant to drink pots of ale in the ale-house at the week-end. As for girls, they came round him like butterflies.

Then Storm remembered how there had been poor harvests in the island for three years running; and how some of the old and sickly folk had died before Yule; and how it had pierced him to the heart to see the thin white children on the summer hills.

He said, 'I would be glad of a good harvest in the island.'

The lord nodded. The lady smiled. The dancers applauded.

Storm went on recklessly, 'And I wish there was no poverty in the crofts, and less hard work . . .' Then he checked himself for his rashness and folly; for how can bread be harvested except by sweat and endless labour?

The lord nodded again. 'That will happen, too,' he said. He rose from the high seat. 'Farewell,' he said. 'I hope you will not be too tired for your work in the morning . . .' He smiled, and his lady smiled, and the dancers clapped their hands all about Storm.

'O no,' said Storm. 'I could play for ever. But now I must go. I expect Gavin – he's my friend, he's a fiddler too – I expect Gavin is waiting for me on the road outside.'

He was led along the corridor. The great stone door swung open. Storm stepped out into the glimmer of pre-dawn.

Gavin rose every morning, grumbling, and did his work on the croft, and went to bed again as soon as it was dark. There were – thank goodness – occasional breaks in the monotony – as when he took his fiddle to the ale-house on Saturday nights, or to a wedding here and there in the winter time, or to a harvest home, or to the agricultural fair in Hamnavoe. Then Gavin was plied with ale and pennies, and came home ox-merry to his grumbling parents; and went to bed; and rose up at dawn to another day of ploughing or peat-cutting.

So the years passed.

The memory of Storm Kolson paled in his mind. He had

liked Storm well enough, though he was jealous of him. But soon it became apparent to him that the disappearance of Storm was actually a godsend. He was now the most sought after fiddler in Hellya. Whereas, before, Storm had got the shillings and Gavin the pennies for making music at barn dances, now Gavin got sixpences and some apprentice scratcher and scraper from a croft on the hill got ha'pennies and occasional kicks.

Storm's disappearance had caused a great sensation for two or three weeks. The islanders had searched the coast for him, and looked into quarries, and probed every pool and bog. They did not, of course, believe Gavin's story of the music from inside the knoll; they put that down to the fact that Gavin had drunk too much ale at the wedding. One wicked old harridan called Madge Bellyon whispered that Gavin must have murdered Storm and buried him in the peatbog; but a letter from the Hamnavoe lawyer quickly silenced her.

Gradually, as the years passed, the island forgot about Storm. One or two ageing people would say, 'Ah, they don't make music now like they did in Storm Kolson's day . . .' But that is the way of all ageing people everywhere. And the mention of the name – Storm Kolson – meant nothing to the young islanders.

Day after day, season after season, year after year, Gavin did the same thing – he went to bed about sunset, and rose about dawn, and toiled in barn and stable and field, and played his fiddle at certain times. His mother died one winter, his father two summers after that, and Gavin worked the croft alone. He sometimes made overtures and proposals to this neighbouring lass and that, but one and all they turned him down. Then, one day, a tinker came to Gavin's croft with a bag of trinkets and haberdashery on his back, and when he went away again ten minutes later he had succeeded, by a mixture of cajolery, flattery, and dark suggestions, in selling Gavin a mirror and a brace of coloured ribbons. With the ribbons Gavin hoped to woo Jemima Scad, the girl from the croft beyond the burn, who had up to now steadfastly refused him. But when Gavin flashed a look into the mirror and saw his grey-stubbled ugliness, he knew that Jemima, and every other female in the island, would refuse him for ever. He was an old man, he realized. He was fifty years old (people aged quickly in those days). It was twenty-five years since his friend and fellow-fiddler Storm Kolson had vanished into the hill. 'There is no end of labour,' he muttered. 'All is vanity and vexation of spirit . . .'

His fiddle warped slowly on the wall.

A girl died that summer in a croft down at the shore. (This was always happening in the islands – a young person would suddenly be filled with restlessness and yearnings – her cheeks would flush; her eyes glitter; she would taste honey and salt, and look on the wild flowers of summer, as if she could never have enough of them. All her lifetime of ripening and maturity and age was consumed in a few fleeting hectic months. Then suddenly she wilted and died . . .) To such a shrouding and wake Gavin was summoned one evening. Between the death and the burial several nights were given over to the vigil beside the corpse, and these long watches were not melancholy – they were enlivened by story-telling, drinking, smoking, games of cards, and an occasional tune on the fiddle.

Gavin, having milked the cow and fed the pigs, splashed his face in cold water and put on his dark suit. He took his fiddle down from its hook on the wall and set out after midnight.

A week had passed since he had seen his sentenced face in the tinker's mirror: he was to be imprisoned in bachelorhood for ever. The gall was in him. He had only death to look forward to, after some more years of hard lonely labour. That – he reflected as he trudged along the road – was what life was, essentially: pain and toil. Youth with its passions and marvels – the innocence of childhood – these were shadows. He crossed the rise and walked towards the glimmering knolls.

The midsummer sun would soon be rising. The first flush was in the east.

A voice fell like dew on his ears: 'The best way to get a girl, Gavin, is to kiss her when she isn't looking . . .'

Gavin peered into the face of a young stranger who, like himself, was carrying a fiddle.

'What's this?' said Gavin. 'Who are you? Are you going to the death-house too?'

'Death-house?' said the young man whose hair was like a spilling of sunlight. 'We've just come from a wedding. But I suppose we musicians are needed always where there's death and birth and love. Come on then, Gavin. That wine has put marvellous life into me. And the bread. I'm as gay as a stallion in a March wind.'

Gavin wondered how the young man happened to know his name.

'Who is dead?' said the stranger. 'I didn't know that there was a death in the island. What old man has gone into silence?'

Gavin said it was no old man, or old woman either – it was a bonny young lass, Ellen of Netherquoy.

The stranger stood still on the road. 'Ellen?' he said. 'I've never heard of *her*. I know all the folk at Netherquoy – Bessie and James and old Jock and Irma. Who is this Ellen?'

The first light of dawn began to seep between the clouds and the low hill.

The young man was plainly puzzled. His face stilled with sorrow, all the same, for an untimely death.

'Ellen is James's eldest daughter,' said Gavin. 'Everybody knows that.'

'Gavin,' cried the young man as the light grew, 'how old and ill and tired you look! That wedding – it's taken a lot out of you!'

Who wouldn't be astonished if his memory was brutally rifled – if from all the rags and clutter of twenty-five years a shining half-forgotten image was lifted into the light?

'Storm Kolson!' cried Gavin. 'Where have you been? What happened to you at all . . .?'

Together the old fiddler and the young fiddler went on to the house of mourning, and as they went Storm and Gavin mingled their wondering voices.

There the tale stops abruptly. The story-tellers did not seem to be interested in what happened afterwards to Storm. The entombment and resurrection of the fiddler, and the fact that the vanished years had worked no change in him – that was all that interested them. The story-tellers left many fascinating questions unanswered. Did Storm marry and grow old and die, like everybody else in the island? If so, did the vanished twenty-five years put sudden furrows on his face, and a hook on his shoulders, that same morning as he walked to Netherquoy with Gavin, so that it was two grizzled fiddlers who knocked at the dark door? Or had the magical food and drink put timelessness on him, so that he was a young man for ever – a lyrical statue among perpetual witherings? If so, that might have been the greatest burden of all to bear.

But it did not happen that way. The island is rich now, with big farms and cars and television aerials. They have love and birth and death and fruition explained to them in newspapers, coldly. The people are healthier and they live longer. But Storm and his music have long since vanished.

2 The King in rags

A young king came to the throne of Scotland. After a year
or two of pomp and ceremony, fine foods and silks and
flattery, he began to wonder how it was with the people he
was ruling over. Did they eat salmon and venison too, and
drink red wine, and sleep on down pillows? More important, were they truly happy?

Of course they were, said the statesmen and the courtiers
– the young king ruled over a contented prosperous people.

The king was not entirely satisfied. He had seen stick-thin
arms pleading at the gate of his palace. He heard one winter

that there was much starvation in the north-east; the rain had rotted the barley-harvest.

But no, said the dukes, the folk were happy in spite of individual misfortunes and communal misfortunes. The king should not worry his head about such things. If there was any worrying to be done, that burden was borne by others.

Still the king was not satisfied.

One evening he sent his courtiers away. He wanted to be alone, he said. He had important things to do, and he had to do them alone.

Once the last scented nobleman was out of the chamber, the king rang a bell, and a bundle was brought in to him by an old man and laid at his feet. The king at once took off his fine silken clothes and untied the bundle and put on (with some difficulty, because he was always dressed by other hands) moleskin trousers, and a thick homespun jacket, and a woollen bonnet: the kind of dress that decent workingmen wore in the capital.

Again the king rang the bell. The old man returned, and led him by a secret passage to an exit beyond the high wall of the palace. There the king in his workman's clothes mingled with hundreds of other citizens, none of whom recognized him. The king as he went along was inclined to be clumsy on the steep cobbled street, because he was used to walking on carpets and parquet floors, and once or twice he jostled a passer-by. Sometimes the offending party would smile reassuringly back at him, and sometimes he was given glares and muttered curses.

He descended steep steps into a tavern, and asked for ale at a dark counter. The tavern was full of men, drinking and talking and discussing matters of interest. No attention was paid to the newcomer.

The landlord put a frothing mug of ale in front of the king, and said, 'A penny.' He looked suspiciously at the silver coin his customer set on the counter, bit it, put it into a drawer, and spent a grumbling time raking about for a small mountain of coppers in change. What workingman ever offered silver for his drink?

In the meantime the king was listening to the talk at the next table. He thought that drink always made folk happy and carefree, but those subjects of his were grumbling over their mugs. 'Hard times, hard times . . .' This new tax, how could they ever afford to pay it, coming on top of that other tax the winter before, and the drop in wages? Oh yes, and the high price of bread and beef. It was all because of the wars against the English. What good did the wars ever do to them? It was a game that the gentry played when they got tired of hawking and playing at chess – that was war. But when it came to paying for the wars, then it was the common folk who had to foot the bill.

'Ah,' said an old man. 'It was aye the same. But in the olden times the king saw to it that the common folk weren't oppressed. Ay, the king was aye a friend and a father to his folk. The king kept the nobles and the knights in their place.'

'But the present king,' said another drinker, 'he's hardly more than a boy. They keep him cloistered there in the palace. What does he know about the troubles and angers of his people?'

The king leaned over the counter and told the landlord to give all of his customers a mug of his very best ale. He left more than sufficient money on the counter. Then he went out into the hard hurtful light.

He knocked seven times on a blank wall.

The old man was waiting behind the secret door. He opened. Together – the old man in front, bearing a candle – they returned to the throne-room. There the king stripped off his common clothes and resumed his silk.

The old man carried the bundle away.

23

The king sat down on his throne and rang another bell. Singly, and in groups, his courtiers returned from their girl-friends, their claret and apples, their games of chess. One of them stifled a yawn; there was still a long evening of lutes and dancing and jokes before midnight and his majesty's bedtime.

'Gentlemen,' said the king in an angry voice, 'all is not well with our country!'

It was said that the king, in the course of time, visited most parts of his kingdom in disguise, in order to find out how the people really lived and what they really thought of the king and the church and the way they were governed.

He went to a seaport and – dressed as a pilot – watched cargoes being loaded and unloaded. He saw the scabs on the seamen's flesh caused through bad food when they were compelled to be at sea for a long time. He heard them cursing in their forthright way skippers and merchants and bankers and king. Then they would suddenly forget their anger and begin to sing together as they swung the cargo ashore.

He sat among fishing bothies on the east coast and saw for himself the hard life that fishermen lead, and the poor reward they get for all their dangerous labour on the sea. By the time all dues and taxes are paid, perhaps one fish out of seven is theirs. They grumbled, as they baited their lines, about the fishmongers and the lairds, the boat-builders and the tax-men. 'And yet,' said one old fisherman, 'we should be glad that God has given us the strength and the skill to catch fish. God loves fishermen more than other men. Look how he honoured St Peter and our own St Andrew. Maybe we fishermen are having a bad time of it now, but we're not being entirely forgotten. The king – he's our friend, he'll see to it that justice is done.'

'The king!' said another, and sneered. 'The king knows nothing about it! What does the king know about the troubles of poor fishermen? Has he ever had so much as a hook stuck in his finger?'

'You're right,' said another. 'The king doesn't eat our poor kind of fish. The king eats salmon soused in white wine, caught by the royal anglers.'

'God bless him all the same,' said the old fisherman.

The king, who was dressed that day like a beachcomber, gave the old one a gold coin and told him to share it with the others.

'Well,' said the old man after a startled second, as he passed the heavy gleaming round among his friends, 'I didn't know beachcombing paid as well as that!'

When they looked round again, the beachcomber-king was no longer there.

He was on his way back to the palace on horseback, taking his anger and grief with him.

In the course of the following year the throne was often empty, sometimes for days on end, sometimes for weeks. The courtiers didn't know what to make of it. Some of them said the king must have taken to religion – he was making regular retreats to some monastery in the Borders. Some were of the opinion he was having secret state talks in the Baltic or in Spain. Others whispered that he had contracted a mortal sickness; he had to take the waters at some ancient well if his life was to be saved.

In fact, the king in varying guises was trying to experience the tumultuous life of his realm.

He came by night to a weaver's shop on the outskirts of the city. He brought a letter and ten guineas enclosed in it. 'Come in, come in,' said the weaver. 'Come in out of the rain. I am to employ you in consideration of the sum of ten guineas in gold. So this letter says. You'll have to work hard here, my lad. No slacking. No slinking off to ale-houses in the afternoon.'

25

And work hard the king had to, as well as the other journeymen and apprentices. People came from castle and abbey with orders for fine cloth. The weaver's counter rang regularly with crowns and guineas. Then off he would scuttle at once to some banker to invest it for him before he was robbed or felt tempted to give some away to the poor.

But in spite of his wealth and his twenty clacking looms the old creature was forever grumbling. The hill farmers – such prices they were charging this autumn for their wool! The clergy nowadays – they didn't know how to cover the walls of their churches with good tapestries – not like the priests of former times! The shepherds – worms were getting into the fleeces that never used to get into them ... In fact, according to the weaver, the whole nation was going to wrack and ruin as fast as it could go. The authorities seemed powerless; no wonder – the king was a useless young fop ... Then a merchant or a canon would come to the door wanting a tapestry or a carpet, and chinking money; and the eyes of the old one would gleam ...

A baker in the vennel under the castle received one day a new workman. 'Let me see you,' said the baker. 'Ten guineas for turning a useless-looking creature like you into a master-baker is an insult. Do you know who I am? Fergus, the best baker in the kingdom. I bake the best cakes that his majesty eats for supper. So roll up your sleeves, my lad, and get down to that bucket of dough. Put bad yeast in, or burn the crust too black, and I'll thrash you within an inch of your life. Ten guineas, that's nothing! Have you scrubbed the dirt from your finger-nails? Let me catch you nibbling a roll or picking a currant out of a bun, mister flour-face, and I'll kick you black and blue ...'

The truth was that the master-baker raged so much, from early morning to night, in the heat and glow of the ovens, that the workers paid little attention to him. They even

26

laughed when he grew purple in the face about the iniquities of the age. For the farmers, according to him, were neglecting their oatfields in favour of raising sheep and pigs and cows, and where would the nation be if there was no bread? The miller – he'd better not speak about that scoundrel of a miller at all, otherwise he might burst a blood-vessel. But the miller in his opinion was the biggest scoundrel unhung. Did his employees realize (he shouted) what the latest trend was? If they didn't they should, for it would spell the ruin of themselves and their families. The latest thing was for the women in the High Street – those grand hoity-toity dames – actually to bake their own bread! It should not be allowed. There should be an act of parliament to protect poor bakers. But then, with a king on the throne like that young hunter and hawker and lute-player, what could they really expect?

The first journeyman and two apprentices brought from the oven a long fragrant smoking loaf with a golden crust on it.

So three days went past, during which the apprentice was put to work for the journeyman confectioner.

The master-baker went continually from oven to bench to shop, seeing that everything was going well. On the third morning he visited the oven where the cakes were being baked. He stood still for a full half-minute. Then he yelled and quivered and flung himself on his new apprentice. 'Fool!' he shouted. 'Dolt! Idiot! . . .' All work in the bakehouse came to a stop. The young man staggered back from a blow on the face. The baker pointed with a trembling forefinger at the bucket where the plum-pudding was being mixed. The ten-guinea apprentice, it seemed, had been shaking plum-stones instead of almonds into the rich brown dough – he had caught him in the very act.

'Go!' he shouted. 'Get out! A baker! You would never make a baker in a thousand years! You fool – what am I to say to the keeper of the king's larder when his man comes for the plum-pudding at six? Would you choke the king with stones? Do you want me hung? Never darken this door again! Go before I break you in a hundred pieces!'

The king had been a baker for only half a week.

That night a white shaking ghost followed the old man through the secret door that led from the stews to the throne-room.

A beggar appeared in one of the city streets – a woebegone decrepit creature with a patch over his eye and only one arm. He squatted down on the pavement with his cap held out for alms. 'Mercy,' he intoned. 'Have pity, good people. Give me alms, for the love of God!'

A group of housewives came out of their houses to pump water from the well into their buckets.

'I see,' said one housewife, 'that we have a new beggar in the neighbourhood.'

'As if there weren't enough of them already,' said another.

'He doesn't look much like a beggar to me,' said a third. 'Look how fresh and clean his skin is!'

The housewives all came and stood about the beggar.

'And there's no smell with him. All beggars stink. In fact his breath is more like a rose-garden.'

'Listen to the way he begs. Did you ever hear such cut-glass speech?'

'If you ask me, the man's a fraud. He's trying to squeeze money out of poor folk by false pretences.'

The housewives crowded even closer about the beggar. One virago reached out and snatched the patch from the beggar's face. Instead of a scar a beautiful frightened eye looked at them.

'Lost your arm, have you, in the wars?' shouted another woman, and whipped the beggar's jacket away at the shoulder. Underneath the empty sleeve was a strong clean limb.

Then the housewives set upon the beggar-man and they drove him from the street with sticks and stones. When they had seen him off they came back, red-faced, to the dripping water-spout.

But worse was awaiting the imposter in the next street, when twilight came down and the watchman with his lanterns set out on his rounds.

The other city beggars had got word that a new beggar, a totally unauthorized beggar, not a beggar of their exclusive brotherhood, had begun to operate in the city. They decided to take action. One of their spies located the strange beggar sitting under the barber's pole. There, in the first darkness, they fell on him with crutches and wooden legs and spittings and hideous tongueless curses.

It was a sadly battered imposter that arrived, before midnight, at the secret entrance and put, feebly, the seven-fold knock on the stone.

The noblemen and magnates of Scotland began now to be very worried indeed about the mysterious behaviour of their king. Such royal neglect of duty had never been heard of before. Where did the king disappear to from time to time without telling them? There were rumours abroad that the king was attending witch covens in the wood. The court throbbed with disquiet like a beehive. There were rumours that the king had a sweetheart somewhere in Strathclyde; naturally his majesty wished to be in the company of this beautiful girl – without anybody else knowing about the affair – as often as possible.

It was this last rumour that stirred the nobles to action. From such an alliance would come nothing but jealousy, suspicion, perhaps even civil war. Though each of these nobles would have given his castle and swans away to have his daughter on the throne as consort, they knew that, for the safety of the state, the queen-to-be must be a foreign princess.

In the palace that springtime were secret hurried consultations – the nobles whispered behind curtains – they despatched horsemen here and there. The archbishop came, and listened gravely, and nodded his head. The court poet was instructed to begin work on an epithalamium. The lord high treasurer said that taxes would have to be increased in order to pay for such magnificent ceremony. Finally a ship with three envoys left Leith for France.

The king had the throne-room to himself for days, while all that agitation went on around him. He yawned and played at vingt-et-un with the royal falconer and the master of the music.

At last one fine summer evening a herald stood on the palace steps and made the announcement. His glorious majesty the king – let all the world hear it and be glad – was betrothed to the high and noble and most beautiful princess of France, and the marriage would be solemnized in the cathedral before harvest. There was a flourish of trumpets. Then bellmen carried the tidings to every street and close in the city. And, in the weeks following, cadgers and tinkers and tramps brought the news to the scattered towns and villages of the realm.

The steeples rang out, peal after joyous peal.

But when the young courtiers broke into the king's chamber, at sunset, to congratulate their lord, the place was empty. There was only the old man there, brushing cake-crumbs and wine-stains from the king's waistcoat.

A young man knocked one day that summer at the door of a farm in Orkney. The goodwife who opened the door could see that the stranger was tired, and probably hungry. (Young men were always hungry, in her experience.) He asked if there was any work for him to do on the farm. 'Come in, come in,' she said. 'You must eat first, and rest yourself.' She called on her daughter to bring some water in a basin – their guest would feel better after he had had a wash.

The woman explained that she was the farmer's wife. Her man was out in the sty attending to the pigs. He would be in soon for his dinner.

The girl came with the glinting basin and a coarse towel over her arm. The stranger smiled at her. She was a beautiful girl with hair like corn in August. She set the basin on the stone niche without a word.

The goodwife told her daughter to get back to the hens. Then she herself scuttled into the next peat-smoking room and began to stir the broth.

But the girl was in no hurry to get back to her hens. She watched shyly while the stranger splashed cold water over his face and neck and shoulders. He shuddered and groped blindly for the towel. She brought it to him. After he had dried his face, she wiped the last bright drops from his neck, gently. Then she held out his homespun shirt for him to put on.

But she said never a word, though he asked many questions – her name, for example, and what kind of work she did on the farm, and whether her father and the other Orkney farmers were contented, and what they thought of the distant king and government.

She did whisper one word before she took the soiled water away: 'Inga.'

It appeared that Inga was the girl's name. At the dinner-table the old woman uttered endless orders – 'Inga, put more broth in your father's bowl' . . . 'Fetch more salt, Inga' . . . 'Inga, there are three bottles of old ale in the cupboard – fetch them' . . . And finally, 'Inga, you trollop, I told you to look after the puddings. You've let them stick to the pot. What's wrong with you at all?'

It seemed that Inga was not her usual capable self that day. She dropped the ladle once; another time she spilled a white whisper of salt over the stone floor. The trouble was, she was far too attentive to the stranger. She hovered about him mutely, all through the meal, anticipating his wants. She kept his ale-mug filled. She scattered herbs over his mutton. She bore his empty broth bowl away. But she never said a word.

The stranger touched her hand once, lightly, and her mouth trembled.

The mother kept clucking, 'Tut-tut, I never knew a dinner where everything went wrong like this! I'll give that girl a box on the ear! Eat up, sir. There's more mutton. Inga, cut another slice. God help us, the girl's cut her finger next. Put salt on it – salt, then a cobweb, to stop the blood.'

The stranger said to Inga when she came round with the crab-claws in a dish, 'My name is Jamie.'

The farmer said, after he had drunk his third mug of ale, 'You want work from me, do you? You don't look strong enough for hard work. I never saw such white hands on a man. What were you before you came here – a monk, eh? A scrivener? On a farm there's no room for folk that can't work. Nobody eats the bread of idleness on a farm. Farming is an act of faith. You can never tell, at ploughing time, what kind of harvest will come up, a golden sea or a few withered ears. It's the same with the beasts – they flourish or they dwine, God knows how. But it makes no difference to the laird or the king what kind of a year the farmer has had – his money must be ready when the tax-man rides round at Michaelmas . . .'

The old woman said, 'Inga, don't hover about Jamie like a moth. Clear the table now. The king, yes – you never said a truer word, husband – the king and the government of Scotland. There were happy times here when we were a part of Norway. Everything has changed for the worse. Sit over there beside the fire, Jamie.'

Inga hurried to stir the embers and throw on another peat.

'But still,' said the farmer, 'we ought to be thankful. Norway or Scotland, the land must be governed somehow. If there were no king and kirk and government we would be a prey to all the bandits and pirates that roam the world with their knives. That's why we pay our taxes. God save the king, I say. This king, I've heard, is not as wise as Solomon or brave as David, but as long as he has common sense and doesn't listen overmuch to fawners and flatterers I won't complain. I'll pay my taxes. As long as the king keeps in touch with God on the one hand, and with the poorest beggar in the kingdom on the other, Scotland will be well enough governed.'

'Mansie,' said the old woman, 'I never heard you speak so much. It's all the ale you've drunk – five mugs. Sit over by the fire. Inga, don't stand between the fire and our visitor. I'll tell you what you can do now. You can make up a bed in the next room. The poor young man, he's washed himself and eaten and drunk, but he's tired, he's come a long hard way, he needs a sleep. Shake up the pillow with the ducks'-down in it.'

'So,' said the farmer, 'you can bide and help us till we get the harvest in.'

When the stranger was in bed, and almost asleep, the girl came in and smoothed the pillow on each side of his russet head. He kept his eyes shut. She bent over him and touched his forehead lightly with her mouth. She whispered 'Jamie'; he had not known that his name had such music and rapture in it.

The stranger stayed at the farm all summer, and he did as well as he could whatever work he was told to do. He learned to herd the cattle into the byre at milking-time; and how to use the shears on the sheep; and how to bring the dog Glen bounding to his heels at a whistle; and how to row out into the bay to catch sillocks; and how to bargain at the Hamnavoe market; and how (most important of all) to read every morning the oats and the barley for auguries of harvest – the song of the wind in the rustling brightening acres, and the menace of distance thunderheads, and the blessing of the sun on the quiet bronze ears.

But he would not have learned the secrets of the earth so well and so fast but for Inga the farm girl. Old Mansie was too busy to have much time to spare, and the other labourers were a little resentful of the stranger's fine speech and finicky ways. But the girl went everywhere with him, instructing him – with only a few shyly uttered words – in the subtle workings of the earth. She would touch a ripening barleystalk with knowledgeable fingers, or listen with tilted head to the half-heard call of an otter in the burn below. She taught him the names of all the wild flowers from shore to hill. Inga was not like any girl he had known before – she was like a creature of the elements she lived among, as if she was made of the same dust and rain.

He watched, delighted, while she ran one day of high wind between the corn fields, shouting.

Only at night, after supper, did she show a little of the ways of city girls – drawing her bone comb through his red curls and beard. Then sometimes Inga would sing softly an old song about the famous lover Rognvald and his French girl Ermengarde. But instead of 'Rognvald' she sang 'Jamie'. And instead of 'Ermengarde'? ... The young man waited with parted lips for her to sing 'Inga' ... But no – she would not do such a bold shameless thing. The comb dropped from her hand.

'I'll shake out your pillow now,' she said. 'It's time you were in your bed. It's sheep-shearing again in the morning.'

One morning just before the scythes were brought out for

harvest, the stranger found Inga down at the pool with a pile of clothes. He called to her. She didn't look up. He ran down to her where she was swilling his shirt in the cold water, and saw when she looked at him that she had been crying.

But no, she couldn't be induced to say what ailed her. He spoke gently to her, and took her hand, and kissed her cheek.

After a time she began to speak, slowly at first, and in a low voice. 'What a sad thing life is,' she said. 'All summer – since the hour you came to the farm, Jamie – I've been as happy as a bird. But this morning, just as I was putting on a shoe, it struck me that I was a silly lass, happiness like that can never last, I was foolish ever to expect it. I love you, Jamie. But I know little about you. You came out of silence, and you'll go into silence.'

'No,' said Jamie, 'I'll bide here with you for ever, Inga. I love you too. And I've never known happiness like this summer.'

'No,' she said, 'it's impossible. I'm only a poor country lass. There's nothing for me but hard work, and next winter maybe marriage to a farmer from the other side of the hill, and six or seven bairns. Then I'll grow old and die and lie in the kirkyard for ever.'

'Marry a farmer!' said Jamie. 'I thought it was me you loved.'

'No,' she said. 'That's impossible. It could never be. You don't belong here – you have learned a little about the earth but you could never be a farmer. I know this too – in the end you would grow tired of me and my coarse ways, because you have eaten fine bread at your former table, and soon – I know it – the longing for that great way of living will call you away.'

'Never,' said Jamie. 'I'm happier here than in any place I've known. I'll never leave you.'

'Oh,' she cried, 'if only I was a princess! If only I wore a silk dress instead of this coarse thing! If only I could say clever sweet things, and feed peacocks! Then perhaps you would love me, Jamie . . .'

And she put her little corn-coloured head on his shoulder and sobbed long and bitterly.

'Inga!' shouted her mother from the farm door. 'Where has the slut gone? Inga, it's time to churn the butter.'

In the hollow where the pool was only the sun could see them.

'Inga,' said Jamie, 'you don't know what a foolish thing you've said. You are simple and good. You are wise in all the ways of the fruitful earth. No princess ever had such a life as yours. No princess ever breathed so sweetly, or had such beautiful white teeth, or ran shouting into the wind the way you do. No princess ever—'

'Go away!' she said hardly. 'Go away now. Leave this place. I'm tired of you and your flatterings. Leave poor honest folk to get on with their work. Go back to the place you came from. I never want to see you again.'

As Jamie crossed the field to the farm, he could still hear a low bitter weeping from the pool. The girl had looked into it and seen only a country lass with a drab inheritance and a drab destiny.

'Jamie,' said the old farmer when he came into the broth-smelling kitchen, 'tomorrow's the day. The barley's taken a burnish. Tomorrow's harvest . . .'

But when next day dawned there was one scytheman absent from the bronze surging field.

The French princess, with flags and trumpets all about her, descended the gangway of the ship in Leith. She saw before her a young man whose face was dark and healthy from the summer sun.

They approached. The silver trumpet was silent. The king touched his formal mouth to her perfumed exquisite jewelled hand.

3 The battle in the hills

Once, long ago, a battle was fought at a lonely place called
Summerdale among the hills of Stenness in Orkney.

An army from Caithness in the north of Scotland had
crossed the Pentland Firth and beached their ships at a place
called Orphir.

The king of Scotland had ordered this invasion. He said
that Orkney was in a state of rebellion, and that the nest of
rebels had to be smoked out and destroyed.

It was a time when the Orkneymen were confused in their

minds and loyalties. Their fathers had been Norse subjects who had suddenly found themselves thirled to the kingdom of Scotland. But they had held on grimly to their own customs and language and laws; and so now did their sons, with a somewhat weaker allegiance to 'the old song', no doubt.

The Scottish lords decided that it was time for these smoulderings to be stamped out for good.

So here they were, these Caithness men, with their swords and spears and daggers, come to remind the Orkneymen where their allegiance lay.

It is no pleasant thing to stand on a foreign shore, even though you are armed and surrounded by armed comrades and led by a valorous lord. What hidden danger lurks in these unknown hills? Rocks and doorways are full of hostile eyes. The very clouds are menacing.

Besides, many of these Caithness conscripts were still, no doubt, sick after the terrible waters of the Pentland Firth.

It is at such a moment that a man remembers most vividly the hills and waters of home. The last look of wives and children gives him a pang at the heart.

He looks for an omen, some kind of rock of certainty among these shifting times and circumstances. Once his foot is on that rock, once he knows roughly what is to happen (for that has been decreed by Fate long before his ancestor was created), then he can fight bravely and well, even if it is a bad outcome that is foretold.

A favourable omen, of course, would put heart and gaiety into the whole host.

The Caithness army straggled up from the shore. They left a few men to guard the ships.

The houses of Orphir were shuttered and empty. The people had driven their animals up among the hills. (For those who till the soil, war is always a terrible thing. In defeat, their ripening corn is trampled by foreign soldiers, and their women folk are molested. In victory, the young ploughmen and herdsmen are lured away by the promise of loot and adventure. Any peasant would rather suffer a three-year famine than the march and counter-march of soldiers across the kindly earth.)

So, it was a desolate land that the soldiers of Caithness came to; and that did not make them any the more cheerful.

A soldier pointed. An old woman sat at her door in the sun, spinning. Her hovel was set into the steep hillside of Orphir. Here was one so tranquil or so stupid that the coming bloody clash of armies left her unmoved.

It was uncanny, that silent intent figure among the silence of the hills.

The commander of the Caithnessians was called Lord William St Clair. With a few of his officers he moved up the hill to where the old one sat wetting fingers with faded tongue.

'Well, granny,' said Lord William, 'don't be frightened. We're not going to harm you.' (The old woman, in fact, was showing no signs of fear at all. She looked at them uncaring. Red thread issued from her wheel.)

'Do you know who we are?' said Lord William.

She said they were Scotsmen who had come to destroy Orkney and kill all the poor folk of Orphir. That was a terrible thing. But still, she said, it didn't matter a thing to her – her life was almost over – they could put a sword into her any time they liked – in fact, life being what it was, a thing of pain and foolishness, they would be doing her a favour . . .

Her spinning-wheel ran down and was still. The wool had given out. She added the ball of thread to the ball of blue thread on her threshold.

Lord William, who was a courteous and kindly man, explained that they had not come to destroy Orkney – by no means – they had come to remind the folk of Orkney, by peaceful means if at all possible, that their true king was King James of Scotland, and they must live according to his just and good laws. It might happen that a few traitors in high places would have to be punished, but King James loved the common folk of Orkney and would do all in his power to help them. 'And as for you, granny,' he said, 'we wouldn't touch a hair of your head.'

'Fighting and death,' said the old woman. 'It will come to fighting and death. The day will be splashed with blood.'

Lord William turned to one of his officers. A purse was opened. He held out a silver crown to the spinner – a flash and sklinter in the sun.

Down below the hundreds of Caithness men huddled. They were wet from their drenching in the Pentland Firth. Those who had not been sick munched their rations, and shivered. It was clear to them that their general was consulting a witch, and something definite would come of that – anything was better than this silence and uncertainty.

The old woman put the silver coin into her purse.

'You are a wise old body,' said Lord William St Clair. 'And you're right, there will likely be a battle before this day is done. Well, then, granny, who do you think will win, eh?'

He still spoke in a half-jocular way, but in fact he was as impressed as his officers by this old woman who sat in her doorstep indifferent to time and life and death. It was obvious to him that she had a wisdom beyond the guessings and hopes and speculations of statesmen.

The old woman pointed to the two balls of wool at her feet, one red and the other blue. 'Choose one,' she said. 'One is for Scotland, one is for Orkney. Whichever runs out first will lose the battle.'

Lord William studied the balls of wool. They seemed to him to be of identical size. He still smiled, as if it was half a joke; but he knew that Fate had measured the blue against the red at time's beginning, and his wavering finger held in a balance all the horror and blood that were to darken the hills that day.

Then because, in spite of all, he was a resolute man, and knew that red was the colour of war and bravery, while blue was a colour that belonged in the main to peace (sea and sky on a fine day, Our Lady's mantle, bluebells in the wood) his forefinger trembled no more but pointed direct to the red ball.

The old one got slowly to her feet, holding a thread of the red wool in one hand and a thread of the blue wool in the other, and she began to walk slowly round and round her house, while the balls slowly diminished. The red thread dropped from her fingers first. There was still a blue ravel on the ground.

She sat down once more in her doorway, and sighed, as much as to say, 'It will be very sad and cruel and terrible, either way. But as for me, I'm past caring . . .'

Lord William's lieutenant tugged at his sleeve. 'My lord,' he said, 'I think we should go back to the ships.'

The other two officers nodded.

Lord William was all at once a man of reason. 'For God's sake!' he said. 'All because a foolish old wife has shaken out some wool! Let me tell you, gentlemen, why we're here. We're here in Orkney, bearing the king's commission, to break a dangerous rebellion. And we are not to do our duty because red is red and blue is blue!'

The old woman put her foot on the treadle, and the wheel birled round, and green thread issued (the colour of spring and hope and childhood).

Some of the soldiers shouted from the road below. What had the old witch said? They were cold. They had wasted enough time. It was time for soldiers to be on the march . . .

Lord William St Clair did not want frightened fate-pierced officers in charge of his troops that day. He saw the white faces around him, and he knew that his own face was white, too.

The green thread issued, issued.

'I wish we had never spoken to this old creature,' he said. 'The battle today will be decided by bravery, not by the dark words of a croft-wife. We will go now. It's time we were on the march.'

But the common soldiers on the road below were shouting. They wanted to know what the witch had said.

Lord William called down to them that the old one was too busy and bemused with her spinning to say anything of importance still ... The soldiers grumbled and stamped their feet.

Lord William gestured impatiently to the officer with the purse.

They were aware of eyes watching them from behind the rocks and fail-dykes. Once an Orkneyman broke from shelter and went across the hill like a shadow. The Caithness men jeered and shouted. A kestrel hovered above.

Another white coin, a crown, was produced and held before the face of the old woman. She snatched at it the way a seagull takes a crust of bread.

'Now, granny,' said Lord William, 'we can't bide here with you all day. You understand, your foretellings matter nothing to me. I have been at universities in Paris and Wittenburg, where they laugh at old wives' tales. But my men here, they would be cheered if you were to say something good about this day, as far as it concerns them. They've come a long way. They're cold and anxious. So try your best, granny.'

The wheel stopped again. The wind shook the limp green thread.

'In every battle,' said the old woman, 'somebody has to die first. I see a butchered lad lying in the heather. If he is an

Orkneyman, then Orkney will lose the battle. If not, you were better never to have left your homes.'

And that was that. Not another word would she say. They must make of it what they could.

Lord William St Clair and the officers returned to their army. 'We have a good omen, a certain omen,' Lord William assured the soldiers. They raised a great cheer. But the officers, who had heard the witch's words, did not see how Lord William could know who would die first that day, an Orkneyman or a Caithness man.

The army was drawn up in columns. Orders were given. They marched into the hills. They sang as they went.

Lord William soon resolved the doubts of his officers. Five miles along the track they passed a herd-boy sitting on a stile. The boy, a red-head, gaped at them in wonderment. He had never seen an army on the march before. Lord William's voice rang out. The army halted with a great clang and clash.

The boy got to his feet.

'What's wrong, my lord?' said the captain.

'Seize that boy,' said Lord William coldly.

A swift order was given. Six soldiers ran after the boy. They seized him among the heather. They frog-marched him to their commander. The boy whimpered with terror.

Lord William raised his voice, so that even the last straggler in the hindmost rank could hear. 'I must tell you now,' he shouted, 'the words of the witch. Whoever is killed first today, an Orkneyman or a Caithness man, that side will lose the battle. That's what she said. So, what will we do with this lad?'

There was a moment of silence in the host, then a babble of voices. Soldiers, in spite of their trade, are compassionate men before a battle. Many of them were moved by the herd-boy's innocence (indeed some of the soldiers were hardly older than him). And more than a few had sons who were herding cattle on the other side of the Pentland Firth. And some were pious God-fearing men. But the dark sentence of Fate prevailed – it went through the ranks like freshening wind through corn, a dark undulation.

'Kill him!' a voice shouted. 'Kill him! Kill him!' a hundred voices roared.

The captain took out his dagger and straddled the herd-boy.

There was a shocked silence after the act was done. White faces looked at one another. A man was sick. The captain stared bewildered at his blood-dimmed dagger.

'Now it is certain,' said Lord William in a high uncertain voice. 'The victory is ours!'

At that a dark cheer went through the army. They cheered and cheered again. The order was given. Their feet beat forward on the road.

They knew that somewhere among the hills a host of some kind was gathering against them. They knew that this rabble had plenty of information about their movements. Ahead, shadows flitted from rock to rock.

Soon, for the first time they heard the sound of many voices, a low distant hidden murmur. Lord William sent out men – the youngest and quickest and keenest-sighted – to find out the enemies' movements and dispositions. The spies went by wide circuitous routes, and were gone for a time, and came back one by one, panting, with roughly the same story. There was no army, in the true sense, waiting for them, but the hillsides were crammed with eyes and whisperings. The road ahead, through the valley, was clear.

'They are a rabble,' said Lord William St Clair to his officers. 'The difficulty will be to bring them to battle.'

The hills stood all about them now. It was nearly noon. Lord William ordered a halt, so that his men could eat their rations before the pursuit and slaughter began. 'It will be not so much a battle,' he assured his officers, 'as the mopping-up of a few hundred terrified peasants . . .' The Caithness army sat in groups among the heather munching bannocks and cheese; but their swords were out, in case a hill-flank erupted.

There were mouth-wipings, belchings, sword-rattlings. The army was ready to march on. The man whom the butchery had sickened rejoined them. The sun stood high in the south.

An Orkneyman stood in the throat of the valley ahead, watching them. Then he turned and disappeared. The rebels had their spies, too.

'Forward,' said the captain. They marched for the throat of the valley. Their feet slurred and crashed through thicker darker heather.

The officer who carried the purse pointed. Lord William looked. Ahead of them was a woman standing beside the track.

What did she want? It was possible that the Orkneymen had sent a peace-seeker; and had reasoned that Lord William would listen more kindly to the soft appealings of a woman.

But no. This woman was a bold loud-mouthed one. She stood in the heather and shouted greeting and encouragement. The woman ran towards them. Lord William ordered a halt.

'God bless you!' she cried. 'Lord William, am I not pleased to see you, and so many of my own folk . . .! I don't belong to this place at all. I come from the bonny shores of Caithness. When you've attended to the traitors, my lord, I would be thankful if you'd take me back home with you, me and my son . . .'

The blessing of any woman – even if she is not a witch – is like honey to soldiers before a battle.

Some of the soldiers recognized the woman. She had been a farm-girl in Latheron; and then a baby had been born to her, and she had left the district. So, she had found her way across to Orkney, and made ale and cheese in some Orkney farm.

A voice from here and there in the ranks greeted her.

'Take me away from this place,' she said, plucking at Lord William's sleeve. 'If they get to know I've spoken to you they'll kill me. Me and my son. Maybe you saw him a mile or two back – a red-headed boy – he keeps Smoogro's cattle out of the corn . . .'

A desolation came upon the host. The woman had cursed them out of her ignorant mouth. Some of the men broke rank. They turned their backs. They began to drift back in the direction of the ships and the hidden sea.

'Forward!' shouted Lord William. 'Any man who leaves the ranks will be hanged! There have been too many women's words today! We are fighting for God and King James.'

The stragglers were rounded up. The officers shouted. Feet rose and fell. The Caithness woman was swept aside. The doomed host breasted the rise and entered the valley called Summerdale.

It was a terrible battle while it lasted. It was not so much a battle as a rout, a massacre. The spies were true; there was no army there to fight them. Instead the flank of a hill heaved. The air blossomed with stones. Faces and shoulders were smashed. The fists of the Caithness men flashed with sudden steel. They turned towards the yelling stone-thick slope. Mouths and knees and wrists were broken. The army reeled. 'Forward,' cried Lord William. 'Cut them to pieces!' The Caithness men ran and stumbled across the floor of the valley towards the torrents of stones. Behind them the other hill erupted. There was a second stone blossoming. Napes, elbows, haunches were smashed. Half the Caithness men faced one way, half the other. Stones thudded in the heather, leapt from stone, squelched into bog. The captain's fist was broken – his sword lay, a long gleam in the heather.

The stone-bearers came farther down into the valley, first from one side, then from the other. From their hands drifted the grey stones of the hill; the stones hovered like hawks; the stones smashed with appalling force into the eyes and chests of the Caithness men.

The Orkneymen sang to each other across the doomed heads.

Lord William screamed, pleaded, covered his eyes. A stone leapt and trundled across the moor in front of him.

A corps of Caithness men shifted their ground, to be clear for a time from the nagging and numbing of the stones; and suddenly a dozen of them were up to their thighs in bog. They sank deeper, belly-deep, chest-deep. There the stones smashed them. They could not get away. The soft ground was scattered with gasping heads. A few drowned in the ooze. The bog-water had a thin scum of red.

By now the Caithness army no longer existed. More than half were dead or wounded. The others turned this way and that, and back again, anywhere to be free from the stone-storm. Here and there a young swift man broke free. But where could he go? The throat of the valley was sealed with Orkneymen, there was no way of getting back to the ships. There was no point in getting back to the ships. This one and that one leapt clear out of the maelstrom of steel and stone; and was free for a time under the summer sky, and ran sobbing; but he did not know the dips and surges and shifting textures of the hill; and sooner or later he was cut off, and dispatched.

Lord William St Clair lay wounded, crushed between stones. That sweet mouth would not speak again for a long time. The Orkneymen recognized him later by the intricate gold on his fingers.

The two waves of Orkneymen met and mingled on the

floor of the valley. All the green jackets lay prone or supine now. Any quiver or spasm of life was quickly douched.

Then the sun went down. The valley was shuttered with shadow. The heather reeked all night with the smell of blood.

In the Battle of Summerdale every Caithness soldier, from the highest to the lowest, was killed; except Lord William St Clair, who was held as a prisoner. Not one Orkney soldier lost his life in the onset.

But one Orkneyman was to die, all the same, before nightfall.

If soldiers are compassionate and generous before a battle, they tend to be brutish afterwards.

Among those taking part in the orgy of stripping the dead was a young Orkney peasant.

He had sung the terrible song on the hillside. He had gathered and flung his stones.

Now it was time for him to be going home. His mother would be anxious about him.

There were four or five miles between Summerdale and his mother's croft.

He covered the ground quickly, wearing the green jerkin and hat that he had taken from a dead Caithness soldier.

He would give his mother a bit of a scare. That would be great fun whenever he told it in the smithy on winter nights . . .

He was right, his mother had been anxious all day. Even at five miles' removed she had heard, faintly, the terrible hidden song in the hills of Stenness. There was no way of knowing how the day had gone. She was alone. Her son was in the battle.

So when, towards night, she saw the stealthy approach of a man in a green uniform, she gave a low cry of rage and fear. The foreigners from Scotland had won the day. Her son was probably dead. Now they were coming to loot and rob.

She took a long woollen stocking and filled it with stones. She crept round by the back of the cottage.

The man came nearer. A green shadow, he stooped silently between the peat-stack and the kale-yard.

The peasant woman came behind him and hit him with the loaded stocking. She hit him again and again until he was dead. When she turned him face up, under the first stars, she saw that it was her own son.

4 Helen Waters

Far to the west of Orkney – so far that it cannot be seen from the shore of Birsay – lies Suleskerry, a barren rock inhabited only by birds and seals.

Because the rock was dangerous to ships, about a hundred years ago a lighthouse was built there. Today, as well as the seals and birds, there are three lighthouse-keepers perpetually on vigil.

But at the time of this legend, there were only birds and seals.

*

A girl called Helen Waters lived with her mother and father in a small farm in the main island of Orkney.

On the other side of the hill was a farmer called Graham and his wife. They had a son called Henry.

Henry Graham and Helen Waters must have known each other since childhood. But on a certain April they began to look at each other with new eyes. They were seen together often, at the Dounby Show and the Hamnavoe Lammas Market. They sat beside each other at the parish Harvest Home. The old women began to nod and smile and wink.

And in due course the minister announced in the kirk, for the first of three times, the proclamation of an intended marriage between Henry Graham and Helen Waters.

An Orkney country wedding in those times was a great event. Preparations went on for weeks. The bride's gown had to be made – malt had to be steeped for ale – fiddlers had to be sent for – the neighbouring women had to plan anxiously as to how many geese and hens would have to be got ready for the pot. And somewhere among the hills a little vigilant man lived who made whisky in a still, secretly, for fear of the excisemen. A message was always sent to that lawless distiller.

The whole district comes together to make preparations for a happy wedding feast; all except the laird, who is too grand to indulge in such crude revelry, and the poor gangrel whose rags and vermin would not be seemly on such an occasion (though old Annie Fae will get plenty of pickings on the morning after the bridal).

The country folk are generous to tramps and beggars. They know how precarious their own security is. And fear comes into it also: those destitute ones have a kind of secret wisdom, they are dispensers of the blessing and the curse. It is best not to set the dog on them, or blast off a shotgun over their heads, even when they make a nuisance of themselves about the place, which they sometimes do.

The wedding preparations went forward smoothly. The barn was swept out. Women moved about Helen Waters with a swathe of uncut white satin. The smell of fermenting malt lingered about every croft in the parish.

As for the bridegroom, he had one important task to do – it was his duty to summon the wedding guests by word of mouth. Henry Graham went on his horse to most houses in the parish. He did not, of course, go to the laird's hall; nor to the hovel on the moor where Annie Fae lived with her fleas and blackbirds.

There were one or two relatives in the island of Hoy who had to be invited. One morning a week before the wedding Henry launched his father's yawl and pointed the bow at Hoy, the hilliest loneliest island in all Orkney. He took his gun with him, in case there might be a chance of good shooting.

He did not come home that day. The valleys of Hoy are astir with wild fowl all summer.

Meantime the swathe of satin began to be cut to the comely shape of Helen Waters. Several ducks made their last march to the watercourse. More soft sugar was poured into the kirns of seething ale.

The minister looked out a suitable text in his concordance.

The laird smiled at the on-goings of his peasantry. Annie Fae looked towards the Waters' steading, and was hungry, and shook her head.

The first wedding-guest arrived, in good time, from one of the north islands.

The bridegroom did not return on the second day either. 'Well now,' said the bride's mother, 'that's a bit inconsiderate of Henry, I must say – a bit thoughtless . . .' But the bride's father said, winking to a few old men who had come for a first taste of the wedding ale (none could judge it better than them, with their loamy tongues), 'Henry's quite right. There'll be little freedom for him after Friday.' The old men nodded and laughed and licked the amber drops from their moustaches.

The women paused, listening, at their hen-plucking and bannock-baking. But the sound on the road outside was not Henry Graham: it was the laird calling to his hound, it was Annie Fae speaking to sparrows.

The bride looked often now over the sea towards Hoy.

Some peat-carters from the hill passed by the Waters' croft at sunset. They came in to pay their respects. They had heard shooting the previous day from Hoy – cold distant reverberations. But today they had heard nothing.

It was then that a first uneasy silence fell on the croft. The old men put down their ale and looked at their hands. The preparers of the feast stopped their chicken-stuffing and kneading of dough and looked deep into the fire. The people in the house looked everywhere but at Helen Waters.

A lamp was lit under the rafters.

Helen Waters suddenly cried out. At the darkening window a face pressed: an ugly filth-engrained squashed face. It took them half-a-minute to recognize Annie Fae.

No doubt the smells of baking and brewing had drawn her like a moth to a candle.

One of the women went to the door, and ordered her away, sharply.

Afterwards a babble of voices broke out about the fire. There was no need to worry, they assured each other over and over. Henry Graham knew how to look after himself all right. In such beautiful summer weather, what could befall a young strong lad? Henry would be home the next day with fine grouse and hares for the bride-pot.

All the same, to make quite sure – to put all minds at rest – a few of the men decided to sail across to Hoy at daybreak, if Henry had not returned by then.

Nobody noticed that Helen Waters had slipped away like a shadow to her cold room.

In Hoy the searchers for Henry Graham were told that Henry had arrived with the wedding invitations indeed, and had been in fine fettle, and after a congratulatory dram or two in the farmhouses had taken his gun to the Trowie Glen.

That was the last the Hoy folk had seen of him, but they had heard the echoes of his gun fading all morning in the direction of Rackwick. (Rackwick is a green fertile valley in the west of Hoy, closed in by dark hills and soaring red cliffs; it looks out over the Pentland Firth to the open Atlantic.) No doubt, said the Hoy folk, the kind crofters of Rackwick, once they got knowledge that Henry was soon to be married, had set him down at their fires with cups of whisky. It was difficult sometimes – everybody knew that – to break away from Rackwick hospitality.

In Rackwick the searchers learned that Henry Graham had been there, two days before, with a hot gun and an empty bag. He had been annoyed at his lack of success with the gun. The Rackwick men assured him it had been a poor summer for birds – he was not the only one, by any means – the only place you could be sure of slaughtering the wild fowl that summer was Suleskerry, forty miles to the west. Suleskerry would be one wild whirl of birds at that time of year. 'Well,' Henry had said, 'why don't we launch one of our boats and go to Suleskerry? It's good weather. I'll still be home in good time for the wedding . . .'

So they had gone, in a yawl, three young Rackwick men and the bridegroom.

They had not come back.

The men of Rackwick do not show their feelings. They

express their joys and fears in the fewest words. But the searchers for Henry Graham saw in the faces of the Rackwick women, and in their cold stances, what words can never express: the very ancient sea sorrow.

Another boat was launched for Suleskerry at once, in calm sea and with a light favourable wind.

About noon they sighted the rock, and clamour and swirl of sea-fowl all about it – it was as if the islet smoked with birds.

They approached cautiously, for even on the gentlest day Suleskerry is nudged by dark unpredictable surges. There was no sign of the bird-hunters' boat.

They entered a gully, a crude natural harbour; then tied up, and landed. There, among the white-plastered rocks, they found the bodies of Henry Graham and his three Rackwick companions. The birds had been at their hands and faces.

Each searcher knew at once, without consultation, what must have happened. The bird-hunters had leapt on to the skerry, and the last man had done nothing about securing their boat. While they had been looking around, the boat, with the guns and food and bottles, had drifted away.

The hunters were alone then within the huge quivering ring of the horizon.

In the bridal croft it was decided to go on with the wedding feast. The errant bridegroom would surely return some time in the course of it; and then a horseman would ride to the manse for the minister.

Helen Waters appeared in the barn in her bridal gown.

The fiddlers struck up, and ale-kegs went round, and torn-up fowls on huge plates went round, and young men and women went round, faster and faster, in a wild shouting reel.

In the middle of the dance the barn door opened and someone came in out of the night. It was old Annie Fae, who had not been invited. One of the serving-girls came to her all the same with cheese-and-bannock and a cup of ale. 'O sirs,' said the old one, 'I was never at a merrier funeral in my life!' The dancers shrank from her stink and rags. The bride's father approached; he intended to say, kindly but firmly, that really she must go; she had not been invited to the feast; but if she were to come back in the morning she would get plenty of leftovers to carry home with her in her bag and bucket . . .

Helen Waters had seen Annie Fae too. A piece of the bride's cake fell from her rigid fingers.

'Changed times,' said Annie Fae. 'Widows come in white to a burial nowadays.'

Old Waters took Annie Fae by the arm and led her out into the night, and across the steading, and pointed her feet in the direction of the hovel on the moor.

When he got back to the barn, it was as if a death's-head had put a silence and coldness on the dance.

Later there was a half-hearted attempt to get the wedding going again. The fiddler struck up and the young folk took the floor. But their feet were dust upon the dust; and the succulent goose flesh tasted like ashes in the mouths of the old folk.

Just before midnight they heard the sound of many feet outside, in the yard. The door opened. The bridegroom was carried inside and laid on the floor of the barn.

'You should go for the minister now,' said the bride's father to the groomsman.

Helen Waters stood looking down at the bird-scarred face, and she was as white and beautiful then as the folk of the parish had ever seen her, or would ever see her again.

5 The Seal King

One day a rich merchant in Norway said to his only daughter, 'You have reached the age when you should be married.'

'O no, father,' said the girl. 'I don't want to be married. I don't want to leave home.'

'And I am loth to lose you,' said her father. 'But the time comes to every girl. She must leave her father's door and go in at the door of her husband. Certain young men are coming to see me soon. No doubt one of them is fated to be your man.'

'I don't want a husband,' said the girl. 'I love to go with

my hawk to the hill. I love to watch the wild swans on the lake. I love Thunder my horse. A husband would take me away from all that.'

The suitors came – handsome young men, wealthy young men, talented young men. They sat at the merchant's table and danced to the music of harps and pipes in the great hall.

The girl sat among them, silent. She danced with them but she kept her eyes on the floor. Her hands lay cold in their hot hands.

And when the love-sick young men looked again, she was gone.

She had taken her hawk to the hill. She was riding Thunder along the clattering mountain roads. The old peasants smiled at her as she went past, her bright hair streaming in the wind.

As for the suitors, they went home, disappointed, one after the other.

There was a young man in the north called Odivere. He was not so rich nor so talented nor so handsome as some of the other suitors, but he had what none of them had – a dark desperate courage.

He had heard about the rich girl and the suitors.

He had determined that nobody but himself would put the golden ring on her finger.

How could it be done, seeing that he had none of the advantages of those others?

Odivere invoked the help of the kingdom of evil. He conferred with dark spirits. He struck a bargain with the magnates of hell. How it happened we shall never know now, but it is likely that Odivere went to a Black Mass, where black candles are burned and the crucifix is inverted and the Lord's Prayer is recited backwards ... When he came out from that terrible conclave, he had the assurance of his heart's desire.

In due course Odivere presented himself at the rich merchant's door. He was probably received coldly by the merchant. But when the girl, standing halfway down the stair, saw him, she put her hands to her rapturous mouth.

Odivere put on her a bold masterful look.

Later that day the merchant let it be known that he intended to give his daughter in marriage to Odivere, a rather poor knight from the north, that nobody had ever heard of.

After the wedding, Odivere took his bride to the gloomy hall where he lived. It was a lonely place, with no other great houses for miles around. The lady Odivere missed the busy commerce of the seaport, the chatter of the sailors, the subtle speculations of the merchants over this cargo and that.

But she resigned herself to her new life. It was not so much that she loved her husband as that she seemed bound to him by some powerful dark magnetism – she could not explain it.

She organized the work of the household as best she could. Once the pig was on the spit and the looms were humming and the washerwomen were busy at the pool, she was free to walk along the rocky coast where only sea-birds lived in the waves and crannies.

She loved especially to watch the coming and going of the seals. Often she whistled to them. They would pause from their fish-catching and turn their beautiful liquid large eyes on her. The seals love music.

These were the only animals she had now. If she thought of her hawk, and Thunder the horse, and the swans (white splashes on the dark tarn), pain touched her heart and drew tears down her face.

'If only,' she thought, 'I had a child – all this regret would turn to happiness!'

But the years passed and she had no child.

As for Odivere, she feared him a little; and at the same time she felt herself owned and possessed utterly by him.

One morning Odivere announced to all his household that he intended to go on a crusade. He had thought about it, he said, for a long time. There was little scope for his energies on his estate. In the east, there would be adventure under the bright sun. There was the certainty of loot and plunder. Besides, he said darkly, there, in the Holy Land, he might be able to atone for his sins, especially for one sin, the memory of which haunted him night and day. Of course no one dared to ask him what sin that was, so terrible that it seemed even Father Nord the household chaplain could not absolve him of it.

The Lady Odivere begged him not to go. Her life, she assured him, would be utterly empty if he joined the crusade. Her spirit would wither in these gloomy walls. Her only consolation would be the skuas and the seals.

But Odivere had made up his mind. The day before he went he gave his wife a golden necklace as a perpetual love token, whatever should happen.

Then he rode south to join the ship of the crusaders.

She felt, for the first week or two, that all the meaning had gone out of her life. Then a stillness came on her spirit. And then, with spring – she could hardly believe it – a wild surge of joy the like of which she had never experienced since she left Thunder and the hawk and the wild swans. She was young again in the grey and blue and silver light of a northern spring.

She sang to the seals one morning. A bull seal turned his powerful head towards her. He surged towards her on a wave. She turned and ran, laughing, up the sand and the rocks to the herd-road above.

The slow hard cry of the seal followed her.

Halfway home, she looked down from the hillside to the shore. The seals were drifting still through the shallow waters. Where the great bull seal had blundered ashore a man was standing, his hand stretched up to her, in greeting and in supplication.

The years passed, and she could get no news of Odivere or of the crusade. One or two of the old serving-women in the hall shook their heads: they knew all about war and the things that happen in war: no doubt Odivere had been killed in some battle with the fierce Moslems.

And they shook their heads again – 'There's no son to inherit the estate . . .' And they shook their heads yet again – 'And the widow, she's still young and sweet and beautiful. How sad it is!'

The absence of her lord had a strange effect on the lady of the hall. Sometimes her heart was wrung with a dark anguish for him. Sometimes the thought that he might never come home again made her sing and dance in the loneliness of her room. Either way, the violence of the emotion, when it came, frightened her.

She lived much of her life among the birds and seals.

Six years had passed, and still Odivere had not returned.

There was a faint cry down at the shore one morning. 'A knight!' The lady heard it as she sat at her sewing. She got to her feet. The cry was repeated at the main gate, 'A knight!' She put down her needles and coloured wools and ran out into the courtyard. Her heart fluttered in her throat with joy and foreboding.

A knight stood at the main gate arguing with the porter.

It was not Odivere.

'This man,' said the porter, 'says he has a message for you, my lady. He says he has news of Odivere. But every tramp and tinker that passes says he has news of Odivere. I'm tired of sending the liars away. I'm sorry your ladyship has been troubled again.'

The knight and the lady looked at each other.

'I have come from the walls of Jerusalem. I have a message to you from the lord Odivere.' His voice sounded like the muted thunder of the western sea, like cliff-cries and cave-echoes.

The lady Odivere invited the stranger with the sea-voice to enter her hall. She saw that there was a seal graven on his breastplate.

The laws of courtesy forbade the returned crusader to speak too frankly about Odivere and his doings in Palestine.

But it was a brutish picture that emerged from his careful words.

Odivere, it seemed, had done little or no fighting against the infidels. A brief first taste of war seemed to have sickened him. He and his men had soon gone north, to the splendid city of Byzantium. He had covered his going with some excuse, such as, that his services were urgently needed at military headquarters there.

But there were, in addition to headquarters, many less arduous places in the city – houses of pleasure, wine-shops, gardens with roses and stone cupids and nightingales. And it was in these places, in the company of the most scented and notorious ladies of Byzantium, that Odivere spent most of his days and nights. Over the years this cold northerner had gained a certain reputation as a gambler and a breaker of hearts (though the first flecks of grey were beginning to show in his beard). As for religion – and Byzantium had more splendid churches than any other city on earth – Odivere after a time did not so much as crook a knee or cross himself under any of those arches.

The day passed, while the knight told, as gently as he could, the lurid story of Odivere's crusade.

After sunset she went and lit a candle in the chapel, and came back again.

Still the sea-voice went on – Odivere at the gambling tables, the songs and the boastings of Odivere in the wine-shops, Odivere among the little dark dimpling painted faces in the streets of pleasure . . .

'I have heard enough,' she said. 'It seems that my husband is a famous man in the east. Do you think he will ever come home?'

'He will find it hard to tear himself away,' said the knight. 'But his money won't last for ever. He is, in fact – I know it – deeply in debt to the money-lenders. Some dark night, when he can get no more out of them, he will slip away. He will whisper to some ship-master. Then the long journey home will begin.'

The lady Odivere lit a candle in her chamber; then another. It was growing dark quickly.

'I thank you for this news,' she said. 'It has hurt me, and yet it has given me great happiness and freedom. You are most welcome.'

'Another winter, I think, and he will be home,' said the knight.

'As for you,' said the lady, 'it is too dark for you to ride home tonight, wherever your home may be. You will stay here in the hall till morning.'

The knight thanked her.

The lady Odivere blew out the cluster of candles on the table.

'You have told me nothing about yourself,' she said – 'who you are or where you come from. But it seems to me that I have seen your face somewhere before.'

There was silence in the dark room. They heard only the thunder of the sea on the crags below, and, at midnight, the bad-tempered porter telling a stable-boy to slide the bar against the main gate. Nobody more would be entering or leaving.

The knight said that the lady and he had seen each other, many summers ago, down at the shore. The pain of her song had moved him. But he had not been able to bring her any comfort, for she had run away from the seal-dance . . .

At first light the crusader left the hall and rode north-wards.

Next winter a new baby, a boy, was born to a young fisher-man and his wife who lived in a hut just outside the gate of the hall. This birth surprised all the folk of the village, be-cause Norna had shown no signs of coming motherhood. Indeed, the day before the birth she had been stitching nets along with the other fish-women, as slim as a branch. The infant had suddenly appeared in a cradle, to the wonder-ment of everybody. The fisher folk know from bitter experi-ence that the coming of children – though a blessed thing – makes the parents poorer and hungrier, for a time at least. This did not happen in the case of Thord the fisherman and Norna. On the contrary, little luxuries appeared in their hut; a woven coloured blanket, a looking-glass, a singing bird in a cage . . . Thord was a rather lazy young man who more often than not stayed at home when the other fishermen were out saving their lobster creels from the storm. It made no difference – Thord and Norna and the infant ate whether Thord went out fishing or not. They seemed, in fact, to eat much better than the other fisher families. Neighbours ob-served – with jealousy or with curiosity or with smiles, de-pending on the nature of the observer – that often there were little honey-cakes on the table, and white bread, even an occasional flagon of wine. How could Thord and Norna ever afford such things? As for the boy, when he was old enough he ran about the doors like a little prince – all silks and silver buttons – not like a fisherman's child at all. Besides – even the jealous folk had to admit this – he was a marvellously beautiful child, with friendly winning biddable ways, so that even the bad-tempered porter bent down and stroked his bright curls whenever the boy reined his hobby-horse at the gate of the great hall. Thord and Norna were a coarse-looking pair – how on earth had they brought forth such an enchanting child . . .?

The lady Odivere was even more intrigued with the boy than the other folk of the estate – so much so that hardly a day passed that she did not visit the hut halfway down the cliff. And what was this? – the boy had full access to the hall as soon as he could walk – the porter had given orders – whenever the boy knocked the bolt was slid and he passed through the courtyard and into the chamber where the women sat at the looms. The women too had been given orders. One of them would rise up at once and go to fetch the lady Odivere. Then – until her ladyship arrived, no long time – the weavers put kisses and gentle hands and kind wondering words on the young visitor.

Once, when he was six years old, the boy fell ill – some childish complaint that makes the patient thin and fretful and feverish but is soon over. The fisher folk think nothing of such things. Their bairns lie quiet in a corner for a day or two until presently they are mischievous and hungry again. But this boy of Thord and Norna's – he was positively cosseted back to health. It made the fisher folk laugh. It was not Thord and Norna that made fools of themselves in this way – it was none other than the great lady of the hall. As soon as news reached the hall that the boy was sick she hurried to the hut with a stricken face. There she stayed, day and night, for a week. She put slivers of ice between his lips in the early evening when the fever was at its height, she bathed his small white winsome body at least once a

day. She worried about his lack of appetite – he was growing thinner before her very eyes, she assured Thord and
Norna – she tempted him with little bits of pheasant from
the hall kitchen, and sips of French wine from the hall
cellar. All to no avail – the little patient turned his face to
the wall – all this fuss annoyed him – he wanted nothing but
to be left alone. The lady Odivere saw, for the first time, a
frown of annoyance on the child's face. It was as if he had
put a dagger in her ... In a few days, of course, the ruddy
spots left his body. He roused Thord and Norna one morning – he said he was hungry – would they get him a bowl of
porridge, please ...? That morning the lady Odivere was
beside herself with joy. The precious little creature was not
going to die after all. She lifted him up and covered him
with kisses. Thord and Norna turned away, embarrassed.
(The fisher folk love their children in a different way.) That
night, to celebrate his recovery, the lady Odivere brought a
gift to the boy: a golden chain. She put it round his neck. It
gleamed in the lamplight. The boy yawned – the gift did not
particularly interest him. But Thord and Norna clasped
their hands. That their humble home should ever contain
such a treasure!

To love a child is natural and good. The fisher folk show
their love in muted ways, not out of any emotional poverty,
but because they fear that any extravagant displays of
affection will rouse the envy and enmity of Fate.

The old women shook their heads. This would never do,
they muttered. That kind of love should never be lavished
on a child. There would come an end to it. This day or that,
Fate would present a reckoning.

It came as no surprise, therefore, to these old women
when the boy vanished suddenly one day. He was last seen
playing with stones and shells on the sea-verge. (The shore
had always been his favourite playground. He had learned
to swim when he was three years old. The sounds of the

sea were always in his mimicking mouth: the glut of ebb in a cave, a blackbird's shriek, shells' whisperings.) A beachcomber was the last person to see the boy. He said that there had been a herd of seals off-shore that morning, led by a great grey bull. These seals had been there for a week and more, he said, lingering and waiting and watching. When the beachcomber had finally manoeuvred the heavy piece of driftwood ashore – the rib of a ship – he had turned for home. The boy, he said, was standing naked and waist-deep in the sea, looking outwards. There seemed to be no danger. When the beachcomber was halfway home he heard a great rejoicing shout. The sea rang and echoed from cliff to cliff. The herd of seals was making swiftly westward. The shore was empty. That did not worry the beachcomber either – the sea is full of noises – he simply thought that the boy, a sea-hunger on him, had gone home for his dinner.

But the boy did not come home for any meal that day, or the next day, or ever.

The searchers found a small linen shirt on the sand. They found breeches with a blue silk waistband in the rockpool. They found one sealskin shoe trundling back and fore in the breakers, as if it belonged half to the land and half to the sea.

The boy had been drowned. There was no other explanation.

The faces of Thord and Norna were muted with sorrow. For days they went about their tasks like people in a trance. Sorrowful faces came and stood in their doorway and uttered sorrowful words and went away. (Among the fisher folk it does not do to be too extravagant with sorrow either: lest a worse thing happen.)

But the lady up at the hall, who loved this lad so passionately and so foolishly (according to the standards of the common people) surely her heart must break, now that this stroke had fallen from the fist of Fate.

It did not happen that way.

When the news was whispered to her, fearfully, by Thord the fisherman, a look of wonderment came on her face, and she nodded. Then she asked humbly if Thord and Norna would let her have an article of his clothing – say, the little shirt. Then she said that she would like to speak to the beachcomber.

'It's shock,' thought the fisherman. 'She does not realize yet. Soon the truth will take her by the heart, and then the hall will be filled with a terrible outcry for days on end.'

But when Thord took his leave, having promised to let her have the shirt, and the breeches and the sealskin slipper too, she still had the tranquil look on her face.

She was smiling, the beachcomber said later down at the fishing boats, when he arrived. He was given ale and bread and cheese. He told, once again, the story of what he had seen. He had to tell it five times before she would let him go. It seemed she wanted specially to hear about the herd of seals. She was more interested in them brutes, and especially in the great bull seal, than she was in the boy, said the beachcomber.

At last, near nightfall, smiling, the lady sent the beachcomber away with a silver coin in his pocket.

Early one morning, a month after the sea-taking of the boy, there was a huge random clattering of hoofs in the courtyard, and shouts, and cries.

The people in the hall ran to the doors, rubbing the sleep out of their eyes.

Horns were blown. A bell clanged.

Half a dozen men stood beside snorting pawing horses on the cobbles. They were dark with the sun; their teeth flashed in their faces. The porter was weeping with joy. It was Odivere. The lord Odivere had returned from his crusade.

Never had there been such excitement in that lonely

northern hall. Servant girls ran to embrace the horsemen. Stable boys led the horses away. There were excited cries in the early morning, laughter, a few tears.

The fishermen were just about to launch their boats. They shouted a welcome from the shore.

Suddenly there was a silence.

The lady Odivere had come to the door of the hall. Her husband looked at her eagerly. Servants and ostlers fell away. Odivere and his wife approached one another. They kissed in the courtyard. She stood on tiptoe and offered him her small cold mouth. So one offers courtesy to a stranger, between bits of more important business.

The first thing that Odivere did was to proclaim a holiday to celebrate their safe return from the east.

For three days nothing was done on that part of the coast. There was music and dancing in the courtyard. Fires were lit on the hill and on the shore. Ploughmen put away their shares and fishermen hauled their boats high up the noust. The only busy place was the kitchen, where the cook and her helpers were kept at it roasting young pigs, and boiling fowls and fish, and baking and brewing.

Farmers and their wives and children came in from miles around to take part in the revels.

They hardly recognized their master. Odivere had been branded by the sun. His eyes and teeth flashed in his face whenever he was moved to mirth or rage; which seemed to be more often than in the old days. The young children who had only heard his name up to now ran frightened into their mothers' skirts whenever that vivid face looked at them.

Father Nord said a Mass for the safe return of the crusaders from the Holy Land. The whole community crowded into the chapel, but it was noted that Odivere was not present.

Feasts and holy days star the rustic calendar. These celebrations in a poor countryside are welcome and necessary. But once the feasting is over there are bare cupboards to be stocked again, by hard toil from dawn to dark.

After three days of festival the boats were launched and the yoke was put on the oxen. Then the dogs had their feast of bones.

For Odivere and his men it was difficult to return to the old routine. They had been away for twelve years, spending their strength on exotic business. It would take some time for these adventurers to bend their minds and bodies to the old yoke.

One thing was certain, however – they could not lounge about in the courtyard for ever, drinking idle ale. It was a rather poor estate – everybody from the highest to the lowest must work, or starve.

'Well, lads,' said Odivere to the gipsy faces who had gone crusading with him, 'the great adventure is over. Now it's back with us to the old monotonies of sea and land.'

The sun-dark faces nodded glumly all around him.

'We're going to have one last fling, all the same,' said Odivere. 'That three-day feast – look how fat we are after it. It will never do. Today we're going otter-hunting along the coast. That will get us back into condition.'

The Jerusalem-farers all stood up and cheered. Then they went into the great hall to fetch their weapons.

The otter-hunt was not a great success. The hunters were – as Odivere had said – fat and out of condition. The otters flowed away from the flung spears. The hunters grunted and panted after elusive animal dances. At the end of an hour they all sat down on the rocks, wiping their brows.

In the old days, before the Holy Land, they had been able to match their cunning against the cunning of otters, and win as often as not. In twelve years they had forgotten many skills.

It was a disconsolate company that sat among the rocks that morning.

A sleek head broke the sea surface twenty yards off-shore – a young seal. The hunters eyed it dully. Apart from the fact that they could not hit it, it was – they knew – bad luck to kill a selkie.

Odivere stood up. He drew back his arm. His hunting spear flashed in an arc from shore to sea. There was a commotion in the water – a scream – a writhing – a red froth. The seal, transfixed, was thrown ashore on the next wave.

The hunters cheered in a half-hearted way. They looked at each other uneasily.

Two of them went down to the verge to retrieve their master's hunting spear.

One of them cried out in amazement.

He took from the neck of the young seal a gold chain. He held it up. It glittered in the sun.

The lady Odivere was sitting with her women at the tapestry frame. They heard a disturbance at the door. Odivere strode in. The women, all except their mistress, cried out – they had never seen so terrible and stricken a face. Odivere flung what seemed like a sodden sack on the clean pine floor. But when they looked again it was a young seal with rags of blood about its shoulders – a red tattered cape.

'Tell me, woman,' said Odivere, 'what is that?'

'A dead seal,' said his wife. 'I thought you were after otters.'

'And what is this?' said Odivere, and held out the gold chain.

'It's a gold chain,' said the lady. Her face was as white and stricken as Odivere's now, but her voice was like his too, quiet.

'It is not just any gold chain,' said Odivere. 'It is the gold

71

chain I gave you before I left on the crusade. It was to be a token of undying love between us.'

One by one the women left their threads and needles and crept away into the kitchen. But they kept their ears to the curtain.

'Your love did not last long once you left home,' said the lady Odivere. 'How many painted women did you give gold to in Byzantium?'

'I loved you, woman,' said Odivere. 'I loved you more than any of them. And what I did in the east – all these small flirtations – that was natural, what a lonely man is entitled to. But what were you up to when I was away? And what is this?'

And he kicked the dead seal towards his wife.

The lady Odivere bent down and embraced the sea-creature. She kissed the snout and the glazing eyes and the torn throat. When she looked up again her grey dress was all red and clotted.

'It is a seal. It is a young dead seal. But it was not always a selkie. Once it was a beautiful boy that used to play in this very chamber. Never has the coast seen such delight and such winsomeness. I think even you, you evil man, would have smiled to see him at his stories and rhymes and games. But now he is dead.'

The rage had died in Odivere. He stood there, in the hall of the women, overcome by lassitude that no amount of rest would cure – a life-weariness. Nothing would ever matter to him any more.

'You have killed my son,' said the lady Odivere to the broken man.

A few days later the lady Odivere was tried in a hastily-convened district court. She refused to say whether she was guilty or not guilty of the fearful crimes she was charged with. She never uttered one word from the beginning of the trial to the end.

But there was evidence enough against her. Thord the fisherman and his wife Norna admitted that they had been well paid to foster a new-born child that one of the women had carried down one midnight from the great hall. The porter described the overnight stay of a knight who claimed to have a message from Odivere to his lady: this knight had had a seal graven on shield and breastplate. The little silk jackets and the slippers of Spanish leather were held up for all the court to see.

The lady Odivere listened and looked with a cold face.

Before nightfall the district court had found her guilty. She was condemned to be burned to death in the courtyard next day at noon.

The body of the seal had lain meantime in a corner of the courtyard, overlooked in the fear and excitement and consternation that fell in waves upon the estate during those terrible few days.

But on the day of the trial Odivere ordered one of the ostlers to bury it at the shore.

When the ostler bent to pick up the selkie the pelt came away in his hands. He found himself looking at the cold white body of a boy. He looked closer; it was Thord and Norna's son, the lad who for a year or two had put a kind of happy innocent enchantment on the coast.

What should he do? Should he tell Odivere, or the priest?

Odivere was in no state to be told anything. Since the otter-hunt he had gone around like a man half-crazed. The smallest thing – like a jug of milk accidentally spilled – roused him to violent rages. Two days previously he had gone into the smithy where some of the farm labourers were eating their midday bread and cheese, and had launched into the lurid story of one of his exploits in Palestine: how he had challenged an Arab to a duel, on account of some fine desert girl that they both fancied, and how, after a desperate fight, he had pulled the Arab from his horse, and taken out his knife . . . There, at the climax of the boast, he had broken off, and looked blankly from one rustic face to the other, and then left as suddenly as he had come in. Only yesterday the ostler-gravedigger had come on him in the stable – he was sitting in the straw, laughing to himself, and sniggering, as if life and time were a great joke. And he had not been aware of the stable-man's presence either . . .

So the man went to Father Nord's door, and whispered to him, and pointed. Father Nord crossed himself, and muttered some Latin. Later that evening the seal-child got a lonely burial beside the church.

Now it was the morning of the execution.

The roads to Odivere's hall should have been crowded with folk, all trooping in to see the burning; for Odivere had proclaimed another holiday, another feast.

But the roads were empty.

And the fisher folk stayed at home right enough, but they shuttered their doors and remained inside.

In spite of the terrible things that had been said about her at the trial, the whole countryside had come over the years to love the lady Odivere.

There was likely to be only a straggle of louts and sadists round the stake at noon.

But at first light an unexpected excitement broke. The look-out on the cliff reported that there was a school of whales off-shore, spouting and wallowing and shouldering the sea apart.

'Whales! Whales!' This was the most exciting cry that could be heard on any northern coast. The whole community – women as well as men – gathers on the shore.

Every available boat is launched. Every available weapon, even ploughs and scythes, is carried. The boats make a great wide circle round the whales. The women scream and bang saucepans and tongs. Girt with such terrible din, the whales turn in the direction of silence, which is the shore. One by one the terrified creatures hurl themselves on the rocks and sand. There they are cut to pieces with the knives of the hunters. Stone jars are filled to brimming with oil. Let the corn die, that coast will not starve next winter. A hundred huge red whale-steaks are carried to this cottage and that, to be smoked and salted; but most of the meat will, of course, find its way to the kitchen of the hall.

This was the usual pattern of a whale-hunt. But this particular school of whales seemed endowed with special cunning. Odivere and his people tried time and again to outflank and encircle them; and time and again, at the last minute, the whales blundered into the west. The whale-hunters were drawn further and further out to sea. And again, Odivere ordered an outflanking of the school; but some foolish woman clashed her pans too soon, and then the half-encircled whales made new sea-quakes westward.

'We will try once more,' said Odivere. 'It will soon be time for the burning.'

Fifty oars flashed in the sun.

We earth-dwellers will never know the huge sympathy that binds together the creatures of the sea: so that when a terrible wrong has been committed, a single pulse of pity beats through the cold world-girdling element, and seal, pearl, whale, and sea-blossom devise with their God-given instincts that which will restore beauty and wholeness to the breached web.

While man and whales pitted their cunning against one another, far out, near the horizon, one by one, subtly and silently, the seals foregathered and came ashore; and suffered the earth-change; and stood as tall handsome men among the rocks.

They drifted into the empty hall where the lady Odivere lay in a black cell, with chains at wrist and ankle, waiting for the fire at noon. The seal-men unravelled the chains – they fell clanking to the floor. The seal-men carried the woman down to the beach. The host entered the water. They led the lady Odivere to the kingdom of Imravoe, the seal king who had waited so long for her.

Very far west that kingdom lies, beyond the Orkneys, halfway to Atlantis.

As they swam into the deeper sea, their voices rose and fell among the spindrift and the hovering skuas:

'I am a man upon the land,
 I am a selchie in the sea,
 And when I'm far from any strand
 My home it is in Sule Skerry.'

6 The vanishing islands

There is a beautiful island between the Mainland of Orkney and Rousay. It is called Eynhallow. Once there was a monastery there, and a school, and monks at their eight-fold office night and day through the year. The monks were driven out at the Reformation. Crofters went on tilling the soil of Eynhallow, and fishing, for a few centuries more. A sudden epidemic in the nineteenth century decimated the population, and the few remaining folk were scattered among other islands.

Two spectacular tide-races – 'roosts' – boil and foam on

either side of Eynhallow, which is empty now of all but birds and seals. (No rats can live there.)

Once, where Eynhallow is, there was nothing but sea. Or rather, Eynhallow was glimpsed on a rare occasion by other islanders. It had no name then. But even as their eyes encompassed the island and the sundered tide-stream, in admiration and wonderment, all vanished like a dream.

There was a young man in Evie who knew more than most about enchanted places. He knew, for example, that the metal iron has a strange power over the supernatural; a pin, or a bolt, or a knife can control any troll or magic stone whatever.

He must also have been a very brave young man.

It is possible that he had seen the ghost island in his childhood. Perhaps he had only heard the old men talking about it. Anyway, he believed in the apparition, and he was prepared.

One morning he came to the end of his house to see if it would be a good fishing day. And there it was – the fertile sweep of green, the low crag fronting the west, the sheltered sandy bay to the east.

He called to his wife to bring him the iron stake from the niche in the wall. He took it from her hand. He ran down to his boat and pushed off. The fierce tide tossed his yawl like a cockle-shell. He swung and dragged at the oars till his heart was bursting. He took an occasional wild look over his shoulder to make sure that the island was still there. His young wife shaded her eyes anxiously from the noust and shouted shrill things to him. At last he felt the crunch and jar of keel on stones. He rose from the thwart and leapt ashore, and stumbled up the beach with the iron stake in his hand, and drove it into the enchanted soil; and lay there gasping, and weeping with joy, for a long time.

So the island was won for the world of men.

Nobody knows what happened to that young man on his

new island, or what success he had with farming it, or even what name he called it.

At last the Celtic monks came, attracted by loneliness and legend and silence; and after them a community of white-coated scholars that adhered to Roman rites, and they gave it its name Eynhallow, 'the island of the saints'.

There is another island, not far from Eynhallow, that appears and disappears, but it has not been seen for a very long time. Its name is Hether-Blether. The folk of Evie and Rousay used frequently to see it in the west on a summer morning when the fog had rolled away.

A girl in the island of Rousay was cutting peats by herself one day, when a young man in a sealskin coat passed on the hillside. She had never seen him before. The man lingered and they spoke to one another. At last he asked her if she would come with him. She laid down her 'tuskar' (the peat-spade) and walked down towards the shore.

They were glimpsed by curious eyes on the sand.

That Rousay girl was never seen again in the island.

Years later, her father and brothers were out fishing when a dense fog came down. They could not tell where they were. But at last they saw a headland through the shroud of fog, and the boat's keel grated on loose stones. 'Well,' said the old man, 'here we are in Eynhallow . . .'

They beached the boat, and decided that it would be best to shelter in one of the Eynhallow crofts until the fog lifted and they could get safely back to Rousay. But when they walked up from the beach they saw at once that the island was not Eynhallow.

'There's a fine big house over there,' said the old man. 'We'll try their hospitality.'

So the father and brothers trooped over the field. Their

hearts fluttered inside them like caught birds, but they showed no sign of fear.

A face at the window watched their coming, and then disappeared.

The eldest brother knocked boldly on the door.

The woman of the house opened to them, and bade them enter.

The old man looked at her as if she was a ghost, but he said nothing.

As for the brothers, they had no idea who the woman was, but they appreciated her good welcome.

A girl and a boy played gravely beside the hearth: some kind of a game with shells. They smiled shyly at the visitors, and then went on with their game.

In one corner an infant slept in a cradle.

The woman said that they must be tired, after their hard day's fishing. Would they not be the better for something to drink?

They all nodded. The young men did not know why their father had tears in his eyes. They had never seen such a thing before.

The woman dipped scallop shells in her brewing-kirn, and brought the drink to the Rousay fishermen, one after the other. But the first brimming scallop she put in the trembling hands of the old man.

The brothers tasted, one after the other. It was a new taste in their mouths – as if all the precious succulent things of the sea had been made to yield their essence: pearl and sea-weed and mussel. They sipped and swilled, and presently the world was a wonderful place. They were no longer afraid.

But the old man could do nothing but look at the woman of the house, and the children playing on the hearth, and the still sleeping face in the corner.

'My husband and my sons,' said the woman, 'they're fishing too. They should be home soon.'

'But this fog,' said the middle brother. 'Won't they be lost in the fog like us?'

'O no,' said the woman, and smiled. 'Fog, or wind, or wild seas – it's all the same to them.'

The youngest brother asked the woman if she belonged to the island.

'I was brought here as a bride,' said the woman.

Then she filled the scallop shells again, all but the old man's. He had never touched the drink. He had never said a word since he entered the house. Now he covered his face with his hand, and his sons saw that his fingers glittered.

The woman sent her two children down to the shore, to look for their father and brothers who were due back from the fishing.

Then she wakened the infant, and sang to it. She fed it with milk and bits of fish. It whimpered a little. She comforted it. Then she sang another verse to it, and laid it back in the cradle. It went to sleep almost at once.

The brothers, sipping their sea-brew, thought it a simple beautiful timeless thing, this relationship between mother and infant. The eldest brother was soon going to be married; he longed to see his Jean with a baby in her arms like that. It was beautiful. It was fitting and well-ordained, that life should bud and blossom down the generations. He would like it if Jean had at least a son and a daughter – a son to work the croft and the fishing-boat, a daughter to bring the honey of generation to another Rousay croft.

But why was his father – a rather stern down-to earth man – so moved by this house and this woman and these children?

Life becomes simple and heroic when a man has a sufficiency of good drink in him. The woman filled the scallop shells again. But still the old man would not so much as wet his lips.

The children cried excitedly down at the shore.

'What ails you, old one?' said the woman gently to the old man. 'It seems that you are upset here in my house. There's nothing here to harm you. I think you should be a happy man, to have lived so long under the sun, and fathered three fine sons like them.'

Gulls screamed at the rocks. Fish were being landed. Still the fog lay blind and grey against the house, and sent an occasional little salt wisp into the room.

'I am contented,' said the old Rousay man. 'God has been good to me. I have had hard times and pleasant times, but still I always got strength to see the worst winter through. But once, twenty years ago, a thing happened to me so cruel and terrible that I wanted to die.'

The brothers looked at their father in amazement. He had never mentioned any such life-shaking event to them.

'I had a daughter,' said the old man.

Ah, thought the brothers, our sister who died when we were children – that we barely saw – that we do not remember – it is her that the tears and the trembling words are for. But why here, in this house of green shifting light?

'She was good and beautiful. She was a great joy to me and Brenda my wife. Of course she was. She was the first-fruits of our love. I sent her one day in early summer to cut peats on the hill. That was the last I ever saw or heard of her. Later that day she was seen on the shore with a stranger. He took her away from the island. They said he must have been a Danish merchant, or some wild pirate. The old women said, a merman. I thought that she would find her way back to the island somehow. But in the end I said to old Brenda, "She will never come back." Old Brenda said, "What does it matter? You have a son now, and another one coming . . ." And I said, "All I pray is, may she be happy where she is." '

So, thought the brothers, our sister is not buried in the kirkyard at all . . .

A tall man in a sealskin coat stood in the door with a bunch of haddocks in his hand. He raised his free hand. He greeted the Rousay fishermen gravely. Then he and his wife kissed each other in the threshold. The householder laid his fish on the stone floor and went into the other room.

The woman smiled after him.

Two young men came and stood in the door. They also carried fish: one had a great halibut, the other had three gulping cod in a basket. They nodded gravely to their visitors. Their mother went and embraced them, one after the other. Then they too went into the next room, unbuttoning their sealskin coats.

'They have had a great day on the sea,' cried the woman. 'How was it with you Rousay men – did you catch many fish?'

The eldest brother said, 'The fog, it rolled down before we could get our lines out.'

'Then,' said the woman, 'you will take these haddocks home with you . . .'

'We do not want your fish,' said the old man. 'It is you that we are going to take home with us. Get ready at once, before the selkie-men come back. You have been long enough here. I will take you home to the croft where you were born. You will live among your own people again. The rowan tree you planted is still growing at the end of the house. You will die a Christian death.'

The woman shook her head.

The children shouted outside that the fog was lifting. They could see the rocks. They could see the glitter of sun on the waves now.

'This is my home,' said the woman. 'My husband is good to me. Could I leave that child there in the cradle?'

Window and door brightened. The sun shone here and there, silently, through the fleece of fog.

'Your place is here indeed,' said the eldest brother.

'Though it's true we could do with your marvellous sea-brew in Rousay.'

'We have found a sister,' said the middle brother, 'that we did not know we had. But a wife and a mother is more important.'

'You would have a poor life,' said the youngest brother. 'All the old women putting their tongues into you like hooks.'

'I have lived here too long,' said the woman. 'The taste of corn in my mouth would kill me.'

But now the old man wept openly.

The woman took a knife from the cupboard and gave it to her father. 'Take this knife in the boat with you,' she said, 'whenever you want to come to Hether-Blether and visit us.'

Father and brothers said goodbye to her then.

The old man was more cheerful now that he knew he could return and see his daughter any time.

She waved farewell to them from her door. Ten sea-cold eyes watched their departure.

The Rousay men could see the hills of their island – Kierfea and Knitchen and Blotchniefiold – across the water. The mass of grey fog had shifted northward.

The three brothers pushed the boat away from the beach of Hether-Blether. The old man was the last to leap aboard. As he did so the magic knife fell out of his belt and bounced from a rowlock and slid silently through the deep water.

Then the vast unpredictable fog rolled in again and blotted Hether-Blether out in a second; though the sea between their boat and Rousay continued to glitter . . .

Hether-Blether has not been seen this long while past by the Orkney folk – certainly not since fishermen folded up their sails and installed petrol engines in their boats.

7 Why the sea is salt

About two thousand years ago a king called Frodi ruled in
Denmark. It was a time of peace over the whole earth, and in
the northern part of Europe that good time was called the
Peace of Frodi.

But there are flaws in even the best of men that endanger
his own peace and the peace of his kingdom and of the
whole world.

King Frodi's chief fault was greed.

Once, on a friendly visit to the king of Sweden, he walked

through the market where thralls were bought and sold. He was astonished by the sight of two gigantic girls, and he bought them at once, thinking that they would be able to do a great deal of work on his ploughlands and in his mines and quarries.

The names of the girls were Fenia and Menia.

When King Frodi got back to Denmark, taking his two enormous slaves with him – and how the folk of the seaport came out to gape at Fenia and Menia – he found a marvellous present waiting for him in his palace.

It was a huge hand-mill, a quern, and it was the gift of a giant called Hengikjopta. There is nothing very remarkable about a quern, however big, but this quern could grind out whatever it was told to grind. The magic quern even had a name. It was called Grotti.

All the strong men in the kingdom had a go at turning the quern-stones – millers, soldiers, hunters. Nothing happened. The stones were too big to move.

Then the king remembered the two slave-girls he had bought, Fenia and Menia. He summoned them from the women's quarters of the palace. They came, and the throne-room trembled and shook to their massive footsteps, and the golden cup in King Frodi's hand spilled a little wine.

The king pointed to the hand-mill Grotti. 'Turn that quern,' he said.

Fenia and Menia laid hands on the quern. Their fists made huge circles. Stone thundered on stone.

The king clapped his hands with delight.

All the strong men of the court looked a bit downcast. They thought it a hard thing to be put to shame by two girls.

'It is easy to turn this quern-stone, lord,' said Fenia.

'But what shall we grind, lord?' said Menia.

'Gold,' said King Frodi. 'Grind gold.'

(It was, as I said, a period of peace over the whole earth. for it was about the time of the birth of Christ. Nothing threatened the frontiers of King Frodi – his people were prosperous and contented, and they paid their taxes on time, so that the king had no need of gold. But the ancient lust for gold was in his veins. 'If I amass enough gold,' he reasoned, 'I will be the greatest king in the north. Gold upon gold! – I might even overshadow the majesty of the Emperor in Rome. Endless rivers of gold! – in all the earth will not be seen such splendour as the court of Denmark . . .!' So King Frodi reasoned, in the foolishness of his heart – not knowing that only a winter or two before the King of Kings, the lord of the universe, had come on earth as a poor hungry child.)

'Gold!' sang the king.

The stone turned. A few bright nuggets spattered on the floor. A little dust whispered over the floor.

The court jeweller examined his first-fruits of Grotti. He reported to the king that it was the finest of gold.

Fenia and Menia laboured at the quern all day. When the candles were lit they stood up to their knees in gold.

Then the jeweller and his assistants came and poured the precious stuff into brass-bound boxes and chests. King Frodi looked at all his new wealth with glittering eyes.

Then Fenia and Menia were allowed to go to their quarters and sleep. They were very tired. The other little red-cheeked chap-handed drudges could hardly sleep a wink for the massive reverberating snores of Fenia and Menia.

It was the last sleep those two were to have for many a night.

Next morning they found that they were to be thirled perpetually to the mill.

A kind of madness had come over King Frodi. The thought of endless gold drove him half out of his wits. He would soon be (he dreamed) the Great Golden King of the whole world, as rich and prodigal as the summer sun.

The quern Grotti was removed into the biggest of the king's barns. Fenia and Menia were ordered to grind gold,

gold, nothing but gold, night and day without ceasing. Guardsmen in vigilant armour were posted at the doors of this marvellous treasury that only yesterday had been a barn, a place of dust and bird-droppings.

From time to time the king appeared in the door, and he hauled at the yellow heaps lying here and there about the barn floor. Once the throat of the quern gave a cry, and out came a shower of Egyptian gold coins. Another time it gave a groan, like a whole countryside in travail, and a thousand coins of Muscovy spattered and wheeled about the floor. Then for an hour it was the incessant seething glittering dust.

The great bodies of Fenia and Menia swayed and surged and dipped about the thunderous stone circles. It was their sixth day at this bondage.

'Faster!' shouted the king.

The courtiers worked nearly as hard as Fenia and Menia, storing the gold away in trunks and chests and boxes, which were then padlocked and piled in the strongroom.

Outside from time to time a cuckoo called in the palace tree. It was the beginning of spring.

Late on the sixth afternoon Fenia groaned. She put her hand on her aching back and straightened herself.

'What's wrong with you?' shouted King Frodi. 'Get on with the grinding. Get on with the gold-splurge. What do you think I bought you for?'

And Menia took her forearm across her shining brow. Her sweat was brighter than the scatters of gold about the floor.

'Lord,' said Fenia, 'We are very tired. We need a rest.'

'Please, lord,' said Menia.

'You can rest,' said King Frodi, 'for as long as the cuckoo is silent.'

Outside, carpenters hammered new chests to hold the treasure.

The king examined a coin with strange markings and a strange profile on it – a man with slant eyes and a long twist of hair. He kissed it and put it in his pocket.

The cuckoo sang.

Soon Grotti shrieked again with the labour of uttering endless gold upon the kingdom of Denmark.

That night, when all the palace was asleep, and only Fenia and Menia laboured by lamplight at the quern, they began to sing. They sang slowly at first, and with pain.

In the song they remembered their happy childhood among the mountains of Sweden, and all their famous kinsfolk, and the heroic deeds they had done among the Scandinavian warriors, before fortress and castle, and at the ambush in the mountain gorge; and how eagles used to fall and furl on their huge fists. And they bewailed the hideous servitude into which they had fallen. They were worse than slaves. Slaves could sleep. They worked without rest or respite for a king blinded by the terrible fires of greed.

'Now are we come
To the king's abode
Of mercy bereft
And held as bond-maids;

Clay eats our foot-soles,
Cold chills us above.
We turn the Peace-Grinder.
'Tis gloomy at Frodi's.

Hand must rest,
The stone must halt;
Enough have I turned,
My toil ceases:

Now may the hands
Have no remission
Till Frodi hold
The meal ground fully . . .

Fire I see burning
East of the burg,
War tidings waken,
A beacon of warning:

A host shall come
Hither, with swiftness,
And fire the dwellings
Above King Frodi . . .'

The quern Grotti spat out no more gold.

Instead, silently, a man climbed out from the turning stone – a soldier with a sword and a brave bright beard. And after him another, and another. The warriors formed first into a line; then, as their numbers grew, into ordered ranks, until the barn was full of silent menace.

'That will be enough,' said Fenia. 'We can stop now.'

'I think King Frodi will not like this kind of metal,' said Menia, looking at the regular gleams of bronze.

The stones fell silent.

A voice called from a ship in the harbour, far off.

Silently the quern-created warriors departed in the direction of the sea voice. They went, dark and silent, like purposeful shadows, down to where the gulls were calling among masts.

The whole city lay tranced with the exhaustion of gold. Even the poorest beggar thought that Grotti's gold would make him rich as a prince in a short time.

A man was waiting for the warriors at the sea-front, the sea king Mysing. The warriors greeted him with raised silent swords.

Mysing embraced the hundred men, one after the other. Then he set himself at the head of the army. They marched towards the palace. Some of the sailors went with them; some waited behind in the ship.

The palace lay wrapped in its dream of gold.

A sentry at the gate died. Swords entered locks – the gates swung open. A lord of the bedchamber fled along a corridor. A sword was struck in the lock of the strongroom. Swords were struck in a score of new-made chests. Gold was flung about like heavy dangerous rain.

There was a brief shrill screaming in the hall of the women.

But the little kitchen-trollops slept on, too tired to know or care what was happening.

A soldier stood before a huge carved oak door. His axe rose and fell. A panel splintered. The king came to the door. His hands were brimming with offered gold. The axe rose and fell. The king died in the threshold, among a scattering of red.

So, before morning, the palace and the seaport were taken.

Next day Mysing carried down to his ship as much gold as the sailors could hump, and the quern Grotti, and the two slave-girls Fenia and Menia.

The hundred warriors marched towards the mountains. Nobody ever saw them again. It is likely that, stone be-gotten, they became stones once again in the gorges and mountain passes.

That day the people of Denmark knew that the Peace of Frodi was over. War had returned to the earth. They had lost their great king. They were poorer than ever. Grotti had brought a terrible curse into their kingdom.

Mysing the sea king sailed west from Denmark. The sailors sang as they rowed. In the well of the ship was a great cargo of gold. Fenia and Menia sat in the stern and laughed at each other, so glad they were to have won their freedom. They guarded the great quern Grotti.

The sea air made the sailors hungry. In the excitement of the battle around the palace of King Frodi they had had no thought of food. The gold and the slaughter were enough for them.

A still vaster hunger took hold on Fenia and Menia, for they ate more than most, and they had not been allowed time to eat for seven days.

'Mysing, master,' said the cabin-boy, 'my stomach is empty.'

'To row,' sang the oarsmen, 'gets harder and harder. The sea is sticky about the blades. We need to eat.'

'Food,' cried Fenia and Menia, and their voices sounded like thunder upon the waters. 'Food.'

Then Mysing took his eyes from the gold for an instant and it seemed to him that he, too, could do with a meal.

He remembered that three of his sailors had made a sally against the larder and kitchen of the palace, and come away with haunches of meat and flagons of wine. Mysing had been angry about that at the time. Those sailors had wasted their strength, going after food instead of the abundant gold. Mysing had had them hanged in the courtyard.

But someone all the same had carried the meat and wine on board. Mysing saw the carcasses and the silver flagons among his cargo. Now he was sorry he had killed these sailors, for they had done right.

It was a bright morning. The ship rode the waters easily. Far to the west the helmsman sighted land, the north-east coast of Scotland, and the Orkneys lying like quiet whales, and between Scotland and the Orkneys the dark fret of the Pentland Firth.

Mysing shouted to his cook to get the fires ready, and to set out the goblets. They were going to eat. It would be a little feast to celebrate their victory. The sailors cheered.

Fenia and Menia smiled to each other.

The helmsman pointed the ship between Scotland and the islands.

The cook excelled himself that morning. It is always more difficult to cook a meal at sea; but he lit a careful ardent fire amidships, and spitted a pig and a sheep, and turned them above the fire with skilled hands, till the carcasses rained back succulent fat upon the coals, and then the flames leapt higher and the meat crackled and reeked.

The smell drove the oarsmen to great rhythmic frenzies. The ship surged on towards the tumults of the Pentland Firth.

Fenia and Menia bent over the fire with great flaring nostrils.

Mysing returned to contemplation of his gold. He was every bit as much bemused and hypnotized as his enemy King Frodi. (Such is the terrible power that gold has over the hearts of men.)

Soon it was time for the victory breakfast. The cook carved great slivers of roasted pork and mutton. The sailors dropped their oars. The ship swung idly. Only the helmsman kept his post. His vigilant eye probed the gap between Caithness and Orkney. Even from this distance the Pentland Firth thrummed and echoed. It would, as always, be a hazardous passage.

The sailors held the hot meat in their hands. They tore at bone and crackling till their jowls shone and dripped with fat. Fenia and Menia held a haunch-bone each, and their teeth rived away at muscle and marrow.

The sea king's meat was brought to him on one of Frodi's golden plates. And Frodi's best wine was poured for him into a golden goblet.

The cabin-boy came from time to time and slid little bits of meat into the helmsman's mouth, but that cold eye never left the horizon.

The sun rose higher. Flagons went from mouth to mouth. Mysing sipped delicately from his goblet.

Fenia emptied a flagon at one gulp. The great belch of

Menia, after she had stripped the last meat from the pig's haunch, puffed out the sail a little.

The sailors began to sing drunken unseemly choruses.

'The food is good,' said Mysing. 'The wine is delicious. Only one thing spoils this meat. There is no salt to put the last savour in it. I have a mind to hang the cook for his negligence with regard to the salt.'

The cook began to tremble and weep.

The helmsman tugged at the helm. To starboard the rocks of Ronaldsay island ran like long dark swords into the sea.

'Yes,' said one of the sailors, 'a hanging would make a good finish to this meal.'

'I didn't notice the lack of salt myself,' said another sailor. 'I was too hungry.'

A third sailor began to put a running knot on a rope. The cook sobbed louder.

'I am going to pardon the cook this time,' said Mysing. 'He made a good job of the roasting. Let him remember however about salt in the future.' He took a great gulp at the most powerful, ancient, and delectable wine from the cellar of King Frodi.

A silver goblet each was brought to Fenia and Menia.

The hull quivered in a sudden outflurry of ebb. The ship began to be gathered into the furious tapestry of the Pentland Firth.

'An idea has occurred to me,' said Mysing. 'I still have quite a lot of meat on this golden plate on my lap. Fenia! Menia!'

'The sailors should be at the oars,' said the helmsman gloomily. 'But they would be more nuisance than help now, with all that drink in them.'

The ship began to plunge and sway.

Fenia and Menia, licking their lips, knelt before the sea king to hear his pleasure.

'Fenia and Menia,' said Mysing, 'I need a little salt for my

94

meat. Grind some for me. Tell Grotti that the great sea king requires salt.'

So Fenia and Menia put their hands to the quern.

The sailors went to sleep, one after another, as the sun rose higher. The bow plunged. The sailors rolled against one another. Goblets and plates clashed and rang. Sea cascaded in and drenched everyone, but in those days the sea was still fresh, and the hot half-conscious faces found these rhythmic showers refreshing.

Mysing took another gulp of the wine that was full of dreams, delights, delusions.

'The island of Stroma ahead,' cried the helmsman.

'Lord,' said Fenia humbly in the direction of Mysing, 'we have ground a hogshead of salt.'

'Surely that is enough,' said Menia.

'Grind salt,' said the sea king. 'These are your orders. Grind salt until I tell you to stop.'

Grotti went on spewing fountains of salt across the deck.

Mysing's head dropped on his breast. A little bee-song issued from his lips. Then his head was a great hive. Mysing slept and snored.

The salt began to encroach on the heaped gold. The seamen slept, strewn about the deck. The helmsman saw nothing but the tumults and dangers ahead. Fenia and Menia worked up to their thighs in salt. Salt seethed through the spread fingers of the sleeping king. The cabin-boy watched the white mounting advancing siege. He put out his finger and touched it, and touched the bitterness and succulence to his tongue, and laughed.

Salt began to inch up the mast. It hindered the sway of the sail. A little scurry of salt fell at the helmsman's feet.

The salt made a ghostly music among the gold.

The helmsman tried to steer his ship, burdened with its white mountain, past the heel of Stroma.

The salt was in the hair of Fenia and Menia.

The cabin-boy struggled to free himself from that bitter snow. He screamed. The face of his lord Mysing was all frosted. Here and there about the deck a knee or an arm stuck out.

The ship staggered.

The quern Grotti turned and turned, and still turned as the sea closed over it. And it still turns to this day, on the bottom, off the island of Stroma in the Pentland Firth. The sea whirls above the drowned quern that, still and forever turning, veins salt through the seven oceans of the world.

8 The Everlasting battle

There was a king in the north called Hogni. He had a beautiful daughter called Hildr. Hildr had great knowledge of enchantments and spells also. (In later times she would have been called a witch.)

King Hogni had, one summer, to leave his fortress and his kingdom to attend an assembly of the kings of the north. He was not worried about going away; everything was in order in his land; and he would soon be home again.

A few days after King Hogni had sailed away, a neighbouring king called Hedinn – the north was full of petty kings in those days – invaded Hogni's kingdom and carried away the beautiful princess Hildr.

King Hogni returned from the assembly of kings to discover women weeping at the gates, and his councillors distracted and in fear of their lives. The women and the old wise men were too upset to say anything coherent. Yet there seemed to be little amiss in the fortress. The treasury was unbreached, the rafters were unburnt, the birds sang blithely in their silver cages.

And then King Hogni understood. One great treasure was missing – his daughter, and his daughter's welcoming kiss on his cheek.

At last the captain of the guard steeled himself to say, 'Lord, while you were away at the assembly with your army, King Hedinn invaded our land through a gap in the mountains. What could we few guardsmen do? The king went up the stone stair to Hildr's chamber, and dragged her down. He threw her across his saddle, and galloped away with her. Then his whole army shouted with joy, and rode after the lord and the peerless rose he had stolen . . .'

(But in fact 'the peerless stolen rose' – all the people of the fortress had seen it – had come down the stairs with her arms about King Hedinn's neck; and she had kissed him in the courtyard; and she had waved a very cheerful farewell to the grim fortress when her lover urged the horse forward . . . But of course none of them dared to tell anything of this to King Hogni.)

King Hogni wasted no time in grief or recrimination, other than having the captain of the guard hanged. His army was ready and mounted. He ordered them towards the gap in the mountains that divided his kingdom from the kingdom of the thief.

There was no resistance at the frontier, nor in front of King Hedinn's great fortress. Instead, a deputation came out to meet King Hogni. Their lord – they said – was no longer there, nor was the beautiful princess, nor were the warriors. They had all fled westward in the ships. King Hogni had come to a naked defenceless kingdom.

King Hogni burned the fortress. His men looted corn and horses, and afterwards brought fire to the rooftrees. There was much lamentation for many a day in King Hedinn's kingdom, because of the folly and lust and unfaithfulness of their lord. Girls were brought, trembling, to the camp fires of Hogni's men.

But soon – once the king's rage had been assuaged a little – he had to be about his business: the recovery of his daughter. They left the pillaged kingdom of Hedinn behind them, and rode between the mountains to their own land. They lingered in the fortress only to gather stores for a long voyage. Hogni took down from the wall his famous sword Danisleaf. Then they rode down, burdened, to the ships, and the shore.

The folk who live on the coast have secret subtle ways of getting news of the whole grey ocean to its farthest shores. A bearded helmsman told King Hogni that Hedinn and Hildr had made landfall in Orkney, far to the west. The king rewarded the old wise one with a silver coin.

At dawn next morning King Hogni's fleet sailed west. The poet in the well of the king's ship sang endless songs about 'the rose of womanhood', 'the stolen dove', 'a creature whiter than swan or snow' – all referring to the princess Hildr.

(But more than one of the ship-masters thought it a strange thing that a spirited woman like Hildr, and one, too, who could achieve whatever she desired by magic, had suffered the abduction. Could it be that she had consented to it? Of course, they whispered none of their suspicions to the king.)

The king sat quiet among the grey heave of the waters.

From time to time he rose to his feet and put his sharp crinkled eyes on the horizon. On the third morning, just before dawn, the helmsman shouted, 'Land ahead!' The king stirred out of sleep, and stumbled to his feet. He saw, in the first light, still far off westwards, black lumps and ellipses: the Orkneys. As the sun rose behind them, the arms and helmets in all the ships glittered.

From the first-met farmers and fishermen in the Orkney island where they made land, King Hogni heard that indeed there was a foreign army in the islands. It had landed the previous week. Yet the commander and his men (said their informants) had been courteous quiet folk, and hadn't molested them in any way, or stolen their eggs and women and corn. In the midst of this army had stood a most beautiful girl – the Orkneymen had not seen the likes of her comeliness and grace.

'And yet,' said King Hogni, 'the worst has happened to her that can happen to any young woman. A terrible vengeance will be wreaked on the evil man who has ruined her.'

'Ruin!' said the old Orkney farmer who had told them the news. 'I never saw a happier looking lass in my life.'

At that King Hogni's face grew red as blood, and he said nothing.

The king's captains elicited from the islanders that the courteous strangers – whoever they were – had finally cast anchor off the island of Hoy, and gone ashore and pitched camp there.

'I hope,' said the old farmer, 'that there will be no trouble in Hoy. We are peaceable folk here. We want no war. You must do nothing to spoil the happiness of that young man and his sweetheart.'

King Hogni kicked, violently, a rock on the shore; perhaps to still a greater pain.

They slept in the ships all night. At dawn they set sail for

100

Hoy. It was easily recognized among the low green islands because of its two scarred blue hills.

Soon, rounding Orphir, they saw the warships of King Hedinn hauled high on the beach. They anchored. They dropped one by one into the water, mouth-high, breast-high, and waded ashore. King Hogni was carried to land dry-shod by his two tallest warriors.

Soon they saw tents in the bleak valley between the two hills, and men coming and going among the camp fires, and a small white figure stood on a hillock and watched them, shading her eyes.

Hildr tried twice, before the battle, to stop the appalling slaughter that would ensue; and all, it seemed, because of her.

She came first to her father's fire carrying a precious neck-lace; it was to be a peace offering between King Hedinn and King Hogni. But Hogni rejected the gift. He was still deeply hurt that Hildr loved her husband more than himself. Nearly all girls find themselves in this position once in their lives; and all fathers have to suffer the pang, usually more than once.

About noon the men on both sides unsheathed their weapons.

Hildr made one last effort to reconcile the kings. She had carried before her by two warriors the entire contents of King Hedinn's treasure chest: rings, necklaces, brooches, all of heavy gold and intricately wrought. Surely no daughter on earth is worth such treasure. King Hogni looked at the heaped wealth in the chest and he thought to himself that a lifetime of victories would hardly bring him as much gold as this; which was being offered now in exchange for a treach-erous fly-by-night daughter.

'It is too late,' said King Hogni to Hildr. 'Take the treasure back to your thief of a husband. I have already drawn my sword Danisleaf, which was made by the dwarfs in the mountain caves, and I dare not return it to the sheath until it kills a man. Danisleaf never misses the mark. Let it but scratch a man, the wound will never heal, and the man will bleed to death. Tell your thief of a husband to keep well out of the way of Danisleaf this day.'

Presently the battle began that was never to end.

It seemed, in fact, an ordinary enough battle, in which a certain number of men were killed and wounded. But at sunset neither side had gained any definite advantage; King Hedinn returned to his camp and King Hogni returned to his ship: his sword Danisleaf had been well glutted with blood that day.

It seemed pointless to both kings to resume the battle in the morning. Not only had they lost many of their bravest men, but the armies opposed such equal valour and skill and determination to each other that no definite outcome could be foreseen.

It was at this point that Hildr began to work her enchantments. She had decided, some time during the course of the day, to show those fools of warriors that love is more important than war; and she chose to do it in a certain terrible way.

She came down at night among the dead men, and touched them, and they turned into lengths of stone. She touched their weapons to stone. Then she crept back to King Hedinn's tent, but he was too exhausted with battle to pay any attention to her.

There was a cry in the night that awoke the whole camp: *All the dead warriors are rocks about the hillside!* King Hogni even heard it down at the ship – the voice of the watchman broke into his dreams. Then the warriors of both armies turned over to sleep again. 'That fool of a sentry – he has drunk too much ale! Dead men are cold and stiff, certainly, but they are still flesh and blood and bone . . .'

Hildr crept out to the battlefield just before dawn, and touched the corpse-stones. One after the other they rose to their feet, their terrible wounds open again. They screamed at their resurrected enemies, and flashed their swords. Then, at sunrise, the battle resumed.

This was the dreadful sight that King Hedinn from his tent and King Hogni from the ship saw when they rose and rubbed the sleep from their eyes. Their best and bravest – whom they had imagined gone with honour and acclamation into the joys of Valhalla – there they were still at it, grey-faced, and putting terrible new wounds on each other.

The survivors of yesterday's battle were shaken with dread. But honour compelled them to renew the battle. And again it went on all day until sunset, with no army clearly victorious. Twice as many dead men strewed the hillside as the day before. As the first shadows touched them, they and their weapons grew solid and cold.

There was small sleep for the armies that night. Never had they endured such a day of horror, fighting part of the time against ghosts and part of the time against living men.

Nobody knew what frightfulness the morning would reveal.

In the morning the stones stirred and stood up. They shook their stone axes and the blades flashed in the dawn. They screamed at each other from stone immortal throats. They rushed on each other once more.

Sick at heart now, King Hogni's veterans and King Hedinn's veterans hastened to join the ranks. Now and again, through the long day, a young man would fall with an arrow in his throat or an axe in his skull. The armies fought on, exhausted and much reduced in numbers. At sunset about a score of living men on each side retired to the valley or the shore. The first shadows fell on the slain and transmuted them to stone. Their weapons lay, stone splinters, among the heather.

The survivors debated feverishly all night – no sleep for them, tormented with stones and ghosts – what they should do. It was certain, if this continued, they would be killed and made hideously immortal. Would it not be better for them to slip away from Hoy in the darkness? On the other hand, what would men say about them, once it became known that they had left a battle before the battle's ending? Better to be stones and ghosts than to be branded in some saga or poem with the name of coward. Dawn found them still at their debate, hollow-eyed. Dawn touched the stone warriors into flesh and sword-flash and frenzy. The living men moved with their axes and shields into the dolorous fray.

After a week all the living men were dead, including the two kings; and Danisleaf was a length of granite on the hill.

But it was not the end, though there was nobody there to see the continuing battle but crows and hares. Under the moon both slopes of the valley were strewn with long blunt stones and brief stone splinters. At dawn, as soon as the first light touched them, the stones stirred and lurched to their feet and brandished their weapons. They mingled in companies, they gathered about their two kings; they screamed themselves into hatred and valour. Two armies, they moved against each other. Immortal tormented heroes, they were flung from stone to pain, and back again. This went on daily for hundreds of years.

The battle might still be going on in the beautiful island of Hoy, except that one day the Christian King Olaf Tryggveson landed there and broke the enchantment; perhaps by simply making a sign of the cross over the stone-strewn valley.

For many centuries now Hoy has been an island of peaceful farmers and fishermen.

What happened to the enchantress Hildr? Nobody knows, but perhaps on a spring night the wind that keens through the Trowieglen is the voice of Hildr, uttering the eternal protest of women that love is more important than war – that when the face of love appears the world is quickened with blossom and fruitfulness and seed, and springs rise up, and time is renewed; but the face of war turns everything it looks upon to stone.

9 The Queen and her Daughters and the Giant

There is a hilly island in Orkney called Rousay. Once it was ruled by a king and a queen. But the king died, and the royal hall was broken, and the queen was left with three small daughters to bring up in poverty.

While the king lived and ruled in the island, he was able to control the giants and fairies that ranged everywhere among the hills. But now that he was dead the little kingdom fell into anarchy. The queen became as poor as the poorest of her subjects. She had to leave her ravaged hall and live with her growing daughters in a little cottage.

There was no silver or silks for them any longer. They had a cow in the field that gave them milk. They had a narrow yard where they grew kale.

The family of women was contented enough, if only they were left unmolested.

But one day the queen discovered that someone was stealing the green kale out of her yard.

The thief came during darkness, when the queen and the three princesses were asleep under their tattered eiderdown quilt.

The eldest girl said that she would sit outside all night and watch for the thief.

The thief came about midnight, and the sight of him terrified the watcher, for he was one of the fearful giants who lived among the crags and hills. At once he began to cut the kale and stack them in his basket.

The girl said, 'What do you mean by taking my mother's kale?'

The giant cut hearts of kale until his basket was full; then he seized the girl by a leg and an arm and threw her on top of the kale, and went lurching home into the dawn.

The giant had a house of big rough boulders. But it was full of rich furnishings and ornaments that had been robbed from the king's hall after his death. 'Listen,' he said to the girl. 'I'll be away all day. There's plenty of work for you to do here. You must milk my cow and then put her up to the hill. You see that wool in the corner? I want you to wash and tease it, and comb and card and spin it, and make cloth from it. Once I get a good thick woollen coat I'll be the most important giant in Rousay. The rest of them go about in skins.'

The giant went away about the rough thunderous brutish business of giants. The princess milked the giant's cow and drove her up to the pasture.

When she came back she was hungry. She found a bag of

oatmeal in the stone cupboard – it had been plundered from the royal barn. There was no hearth; the giants have never learned to use fire; their appetites are huge and raw and bestial. The princess got water from the burn. She found a pot that had been stolen from the royal kitchen. In a short time she had porridge bubbling over a peat fire on the floor.

The smell was delicious. She turned round to get a plate and spoon (also stolen from her father's hall – giants don't need such implements, they eat out of their clumsy hands). The house was full of small folk with yellow hair. They pleaded with her, those fairies, to give them some porridge. They said they were hungry, and they looked it, with their poor pinched faces.

Some princesses remain selfish for a long time, even after they are poor and should know better. This princess said sharply:

'Little for one and less for two,
 And never a grain have I for you.'

The fairies left the house, hurt and angry. The princess ate the porridge herself, down to the last pot-scraping.

Then she thought it was high time for her to be getting on with her second task, the making of cloth from raw wool, before the giant came home.

The wool was piled in the corner like a little bank of fog.

She stood and looked at it for a long time. She fingered it. She blew a wisp on her breath. But she had no idea what to do with it. When she was a child in the hall, poor women from the cottages round about had been hired to card and spin the wool. Such menial work was not for a little princess.

Wash the wool, the giant had said. She sprinkled a few drops of water from the bucket over the thick grey fog in the corner, but that seemed not to brighten the wool at all. And while she was puzzling and pondering, a shadow filled the room. She turned, and discovered that the giant was home.

His rage was terrible when he saw that she hadn't done her work.

He beat her till his arm was tired. Then he bound and gagged her and threw her across the beams of his house, where his hens were roosting.

In the little royal tumbledown cottage there was much grief when morning came, and the queen discovered that her eldest daughter had vanished, along with half-a-hundred hearts of kale.

Still, they were proud people, in spite of their poverty. Their kingdom had shrunk to a little field, and one beast and some vegetables, but the queen and her daughters were determined that there must be no lawlessness there. If they could keep this last little remnant intact, in time good order and government might spread once more over the whole island.

The second daughter said that she would keep vigil the next night.

The giant came with his straw basket. His knife flashed in the starlight. Kale-heart after kale-heart was separated from its root.

'Leave my mother's kale alone,' said the middle princess.

The giant paid no attention. He cut as much kale as would fill his basket, then he seized the trembling girl and threw her on top of the load, and went lurching home into the dawn.

'His house is rougher and filthier than any cave,' said the princess, weeping.

'Listen carefully,' said the giant. 'The last servant I had was so stupid, or else so lazy, that she couldn't do her work. She got her wages all right, and it wasn't pieces of silver either. You'll get the same, you trollop, if you don't do what

I say. I'll be away all day – I have some business with the other giants in the hills. I'll be home by nightfall. By that time – are you listening? – I want my cow milked and put up to the hill. Then I want that wool in the corner – cast your eye on it – I want that wool washed and teased, combed and carded and spun. That isn't too much to ask.'

Then he went away. His footsteps faded like thunder between Kierfea and Blotchniefiold.

The middle princess knew how to milk a cow; she had had to learn by bitter experience.

She set the bucket of white trembling circles on the cold stone threshold.

'Dapple,' she said to the cow, 'you and I are going up to the pasture now.'

She left Dapple grazing contentedly among the lush green grass.

'How hungry I am!' said the princess on her way back to the giant's house.

She opened the cupboard and saw a sack of oatmeal. (Oatmeal is very different from the grouse and scallops and white honey-bread she had eaten in her childhood, when her father was king, but when you are hungry the coarsest food tastes excellent.) She gathered sticks and made a fire in that hearthless house. Soon the porridge-pot bubbled over the flames.

She turned to get a plate and spoon and saw a hundred small folk with yellow hair and twitching nostrils crowding in at the door.

'Give us a bite of your porridge,' they pleaded with voices that were like petal-falls and web-whispers. The princess knew the cunning of the fairies. They were not hungry at all. But if they could get a human being to share food with them, that person would be in their power for ever.

The princess raised her spoon and rushed at them, and they ran away terrified.

'Well,' said the princess when she had scraped the pot and licked the spoon clean, 'I suppose I'd better set about making the cloth before that great stupid blundering creature comes home.'

She had no more idea of what to do than her sister. She stood in front of the rough shapeless mass of wool in the corner. Comb it, the giant had said. She took the comb out of her hair and made a few half-hearted strokes through the wool, but it seemed to make little difference.

Then a shadow filled the house, and when the princess turned the giant stood there.

His rage was terrible when he saw that the wool had hardly been touched.

He beat the princess till his hand was sore. Then he bound her hand and foot, and gagged her, and slung her across the roof-beams beside her sister. The hens squawked and complained for a little while; then they furled their wings and settled down for the night.

Nothing was heard in that hovel but the low weeping of the two princesses under the thatch.

The giant snored for a while after his supper. Then he woke up and reached for his basket and went out.

'Dear one,' said the queen to her sole remaining daughter, drawing the rags of finer days about her, 'you shall not, *must* not go into the kale-yard tonight. I forbid it!'

So the little princess crept into bed beside her mother.

She was much more beautiful than her two sisters, and much cleverer; and, which is more important, she had a kind heart.

When she saw that her mother was well asleep, she crept out of bed and took a blanket about her – for it was a cold dark night – and sat down in a corner of the kale-yard.

The ground shook like a small earthquake. A great shadow blotted out the stars. A knife flashed and flashed and flashed. A hundred hearts of kale rolled on the earth.

'Please,' said the little princess, 'my mother and I are very poor, and if you take any more of our kale we will starve.'

The giant filled his basket with kale, then he took the princess by the hair and threw her on top of the load. And he went lurching into the dawn.

'Look here,' said the giant to the princess, 'I've had two stupid servants here, in quick succession, and they were hopeless and helpless when it came to work. I hope with all my heart that you manage better than them. Because if you don't, you'll end up the same way.'

'What must I do?' said the little princess. 'I'll work for you as well as I can.'

'Well,' said the giant, 'you see old Dapple in the field out there? You must milk her first.'

'I'll do that,' said the princess. 'She's a beautiful cow. I'm good at milking.'

'After that,' said the giant, 'I suppose you can have a bite to eat. There's a bag of oatmeal in the cupboard there. Make porridge.'

'I love porridge,' said the princess.

'Porridge makes you strong,' said the giant. 'You'll need all the strength you can get, too, because I want all that wool in the corner there made into cloth before the sun goes down.'

'That will be perfectly simple' said the little princess, but her heart quailed inside her, for the queen had never taught her children such country crafts as spinning.

'I'll be away all day,' said the giant. 'A council of giants in the hills. Since the downfall of the royal family this island must be ruled somehow. We don't want a rabble of fairies and trows and finn-men in charge of things. Goodbye.'

The little princess was left alone to perform her tasks.

'Dear Dapple,' she said as she milked the cow, 'what

white sweet milk you give! Thank you, Dapple, that's the lot. I bet you're longing for that grass in the high field. Come on, then.'

The air on the hillside makes everybody hungry. 'Some porridge first,' said the princess. 'Then I must do something about that wool.'

She was stirring the porridge over the fire when she heard a rustling and a sighing like the wind through a cornfield.

She turned, and there stood a horde of hungry fairies in the door. Some of them pointed at their mouths and some of them patted their stomachs. Their nostrils drank the delicious smell.

'Well,' said the princess, 'you're hungry – is that it? You want some of this porridge. You'll get your fingers burnt, and your mouths too, if you sip it out of the pot. There's only one plate and one spoon in this place, as far as I can see.'

The host of fairies disappeared, laughing, and came back in less than a minute, each carrying a shell or a hollow stone. The princess spooned out porridge for them all, and there was enough left for herself. The porridge, with Dapple's white milk on top, tasted delicious.

The fairies thanked the princess and went away.

'Now for trouble,' said the princess. 'How on earth am I going to turn that heap of wool into a coat for His Clumsiness? I'll just have to confess to him, when he comes home, that I never learned how.'

She heard a little snigger in the door. She turned, and saw a very small yellow-headed fairy, a boy, giggling in the doorway.

'Have you any work for us to do?' said the fairy.

'Well,' said the princess, 'could you do anything for example with that wool over there?'

'We could make cloth out of that in a very short time,' said the boy.

The heart of the princess beat with joy.

But she knew too that bargaining with fairies, or any supernatural creature, calls for much subtlety and cunning. They propose something simple, but before long you find yourself entangled in a web from which you cannot escape, and then you belong to them utterly, and they feed deeply on the honey of mortality: all the songs and patterns and legends which, because of their timelessness, they do not themselves know how to body forth.

The princess knew, however, that she would have to take the risk.

'That would be wonderful,' she said to the wind-blown creature in the door. 'But I might not be able to pay you for your work.'

'Don't worry about that,' said the fairy child. 'Let me see. Suppose, in return for our work, you try to find out my name. That's all the payment we want.'

Nothing, surely, could be simpler or more charming than that: to find out, and utter when challenged, the name of this little creature.

But she would never be able to find out. To discover the name of a fairy is as rare as to find a pearl in an oyster.

Before sunset they would fall on her, the whole host, and drag her under the hill.

'Well,' thought the princess, 'I suppose I would rather belong to them than to the giant, like my two poor sisters.'

She smiled at the cunning, eager little creature in the door and said, 'Your name – how easy! How delightful! I'll tell you what it is as soon as you see to the wool.'

The fairy went to the corner and gathered all the wool about him. He heaved like a little bank of fog. Wool and boy disappeared through the door.

There was nothing left for the princess to do now but wait, without much hope. She was trapped between the brutish rage of the giant and the subtle underworld cunning of the fairies.

She had another visitor before sunset – an old beggar woman who knocked at the door and asked for a bite to eat.

There was just a scraping of porridge left in the pot, and a sup of milk.

The old woman thanked the princess and hurried away before the giant got home.

The princess waited.

There was thunder in the far hills. The council of giants was breaking up.

Then a tap came at the door. It was the same old woman who had scraped the porridge pot.

'The strangest thing happened to me,' said the old woman to the princess. 'I felt sleepy after the porridge, so I stretched myself out on that little green hillock out there. Didn't I hear voices inside the hillock and spinning-wheels going, and a loom clacking? The folk inside the hill sang a song. It went like this:

'Tease, teasers, tease
 Card, carders, card
 Spin, spinners, spin
 Peedie-Fool, Peedie-Fool is my name.'

I just thought I would tell you, you being so kind as to give a poor old wife some porridge and milk.'

Then the old woman said goodnight and went away over the hill by another track.

Soon there was a shout at the door, and a bale of cloth was thrown inside. The little princess fingered it – it was of marvellous weave and texture.

Then she saw the fairy boy with yellow hair standing in the threshold.

'The name,' he said. 'Tell me my name.'

The princess considered for a second or two. 'Yellow Head,' she said.

Outside the fairy host shouted, 'No!'

'Try again,' said the fairy. 'You must pay for the cloth,

115

you know. That was the agreement. Tell me my name.'

The princess furrowed her brow and pondered. Then she said, 'Wool Boy.'

'No,' yelled the thousand fairies outside.

'You have one last chance,' said the little creature in a voice full of menace. 'If you do not guess correctly you must come with us. For ever and for ever. *Tell me my name.*'

'Peedie-Fool,' said the princess.

Peedie-Fool shrieked. Outside the fairy host shrieked with rage. The noise was like rusty iron on a grindstone, a thing to set the teeth on edge. Then the whole host fled up into the hill.

'I wonder,' thought the princess, 'if my master will be pleased with the cloth.'

She need not have wondered. When the giant came home at sunset and saw the web of cloth on the table he was delighted. He fingered it with such joy and gratitude that the heart of the little princess melted a little for him. (The truth is, giants have no skill in any human craft, like weaving or pottery or story-telling. Their clothes are skins. For them there is something magical in the turning of a mass of wool into a coat.)

'You have done well,' said the giant. 'Now you must stay here always and be my wife. I will try to be a good husband to you, little wife. Anything you want I will do.'

'Tell me, then,' said the princess, 'what happened to the two girls who were here before me?'

The giant pointed to the rafters. 'They're up there, both of them,' he said. 'It's the best place for them. They were useless creatures.'

The little princess looked and saw in the shadows overhead her two sisters, white and bound and gagged.

'Well,' she said. 'I hope things will go more smoothly from now on.'

'I wouldn't harm a hair of your head,' said the giant

humbly. 'You have made me very happy. I will do anything you say, little wife, little cloth-maker.'

'My poor mother,' said the princess, 'who was once the queen of this island – think how miserable she must be. You have stolen all her kale. She has no daughters now to comfort her. Her cow eats the coarsest heather in the island, not like Dapple with her rich juicy grass. Please cut some grass in your field and carry it to my mother's door. In that way you can make amends for some of the damage you have done.'

The giant said he would do that at once. He took his scythe and went out.

As soon as he had gone the princess pulled her eldest sister down from the beams. She unbound her and put some clothes on her. 'Say nothing,' she said. 'Lie down quiet in that basket.'

The eldest princess lay down in the basket, and the clever little one covered her with cups, plates, harps, and bits of tapestry that had been stolen from the royal hall when anarchy broke out after the king's death.

'Put the grass in this basket,' said the princess to the giant as soon as he returned with his burden of sweet-smelling hay, 'and take it to my mother.'

So the giant trudged over the hill with the basket on his back to the queen's door, and knocked, and left it there.

The queen came out and found a basket of new-mown hay. 'What a poor gift for anyone to leave,' she thought. But when she delved deeper she discovered some of her lost treasures, and underneath them a much greater treasure, her eldest daughter.

So the little princess was mistress now of the giant's house. The great blundering creature followed her with devoted eyes, whatever she did. He obeyed at once her lightest whim.

'More grass,' she said. 'My mother's cow will have a taste

for our grass now. You must carry over another basketful.'

'I'll cut some at once,' said the giant. He took down the scythe and went out.

The little princess lowered her second sister from the rafters, and unbound her and put some clothes on her. The hens that roosted under the roof *were* glad to see the last of her.

'Say nothing,' said the little mistress of the house. 'Lie quiet at the bottom of the basket.'

She covered the second sister with more precious things that had been looted from the great hall – manuscripts, and quilts stuffed with swans'-down, and silver candle-sticks, things that in any case the giant was too stupid to know how to use or appreciate.

The giant stooped under the lintel with his great green burden in which a few bees still buzzed.

'Into the basket with it,' said the little princess. 'Then over the hill to the queen. It's late. Her cow will be hungry.'

The giant took the loaded basket on his back and set off over the hill. He saw two faces peering at him from the door of the queen's cottage, and he thought that was strange, for didn't the old queen who had once been powerful live all by herself in her poverty?

He left the basket at the end of the house and shouted 'Here's a bit for your old cow,' and set off for home.

And as he went he sang, so glad he was to be going back to the dear beautiful clever coat-maker that he had got for a wife.

The queen, as soon as the giant had gone, came out and rummaged through the grass and found more of her family heirlooms, but more precious than them all she found at the bottom of the basket her second daughter.

Next day the giant asked his little wife if there was any-thing he could do for her.

'That cow of my mother's,' said the princess, 'she'll never

eat the coarse ditch-grass again. Be a good giant and cut some more of your sweet meadow-grass for her.'

'Well, I'll do it once more,' said the giant. He took down the scythe from the wall.

'I won't be here when you come back,' said the princess. 'I have to go out to the burn for water. You know what to do without being told. Just empty the grass into the basket and carry it over the hill to my mother's door.'

'Very good,' said the giant, and went out to the meadow.

The princess watched the flashings of the scythe in the sun. Then she gathered the last of the loot that the giant had taken from the king's hall – an hour-glass in an oak frame, a golden crown, a jewelled bridle, and a royal coat-of-state. She got into the basket and covered herself with these treasures.

Soon she heard a grunting and a footfall in the door, and a rich smell of earth and wind and sun, and a green cataract poured over her, and a grass-imprisoned butterfly flapped a wing close to her nose. Then she felt herself being hoisted up, and she was jolted up and down as the giant strode quickly over the hill to her mother's door.

Soon the great footsteps lost their rhythm and stopped. They were near the place.

She heard on the wind three small welcoming cries.

'Mistress,' shouted the giant. 'Here's some more grass for that old cow of yours. May she relish it, for it's the last she'll get.'

'Leave the basket at the end of the kale-yard,' came the voice of her mother the queen. 'Then come here, sir giant, under the window, till I thank you for all your kindness!'

The little princess was set down with a bit of a bump. She put her head out of the basket and saw the giant standing under her mother's window.

Then she saw something that made her laugh and wince at the same time.

Six white hands at the high window were balancing a boiling cauldron on the ledge. They tilted the cauldron and a seething steaming scalding cascade fell over the giant.

He roared like thunder.

The whole island was filled with the sound of rage and pain and fear and astonishment. (For, of course, the giants are so stupid that they do not know how to boil water, and he imagined that there was some kind of terrible magic in this water.)

He fled among the farthest hills and crags of Rousay, and has never been seen since.

As for the little princess, she flung all the rich things from her and climbed out of the basket and ran into the delighted arms of her mother.

That is the end of the tale. Beyond it is only speculation. But I think we may assume that, now that the fairies and the giants had been outwitted and brought under control, the kingdom of man was established once more in the island.

When at last the old queen died, who had seen so much sorrow and misfortune, which of her daughters succeeded her? Let us hope, for the sake of the island folk, it was neither the eldest princess nor the middle princess, with their selfishness and stupidity, but the little one who had showed such wisdom and foresight and charity.

And let us hope that a prince sailed in due course from one of the other islands, and married her. And that together they rebuilt the royal hall. And that in due course sons and daughters were born to them. And that they managed to keep the supernatural creatures in subjection. And that they lived and reigned happy ever after.

10 The Trow Doctor

A Rousay farmer took to his bed one winter and did not get up again. There was plenty of work to do about the farm, and his strength and knowledge were sorely missed. What made the situation doubly galling for his wife was that the farmer had no symptoms of illness. But he said he had not the strength to work. He kept saying that he was on his death-bed; the only time he would ever be out of doors again was when the neighbour men came to carry him to the kirkyard.

It was sad to see that strong man lying there useless and

dejected in the box-bed. Soon it would be time for plough-ing and sowing, but he whispered that these labours were beyond his strength now. His young son would have to do the work.

In the islands winter used to be a merry time, with danc-ing and fiddling and feasting; but the death-bound farmer had no taste for such vanity now. He turned his face to the wall.

One day his wife came to his bedside and began to rail at him. 'Ill, indeed! There's nothing wrong with you! You're lazy, that's what it is! You're a shame and a disgrace, lying there useless in your bed and the sun shining outside! A woman can't do all the farm work. Your son is too small to plough. Your daughter – how can she cut peats with her small white hands? Another year and the farm will be in ruins!'

The goodwife hoped that this show of scorn and anger would rouse the farmer from his imaginary sickness. But he only sighed and turned his face away.

Various men of power were sent for. The minister came and reasoned with him. Why was he not getting his plough and his ox ready? – the spring rain was melting the snow on the summit of Kierfea. There was obviously nothing wrong with him, said the minister, with his steady breathing and hearty appetite and thick shoulders. He must really think of his duty towards his family.

The farmer's only answer was that the minister would certainly be needed to read the funeral service before mid-summer.

The minister went away, baffled.

The farmer's brother came from the other end of the island. 'If you think,' said he to the bedridden man, 'that I'm going to keep you and your wife and your children in eggs and potatoes and cheese and bread and malt, you're very much mistaken. You have a far better farm than I do. Get up and work it. Folk are making a mock of you far beyond this island. Do you know what they're calling you? They're calling you the Rousay bear that sleeps all winter.'

The farmer said he was glad that people could still laugh, if it should only be at his expense. Let them laugh – the time for laughter was soon over. As for him, he would never laugh again.

The brother went away, baffled.

'Now look you here, my man,' said the laird. 'Listen carefully to what I'm saying. When I see that one of my holdings is not being well farmed, I take steps to remedy the situation. As I passed on my horse just now, I saw that small son of yours trying to plough your field. I will not put up with it. Either you get out of that bed and do the work you have to do, or I will see that there is a new tenant in this farm at Martinmas. I'm warning you, now.'

The farmer said it couldn't be helped. The laird would have to do as he saw fit. As for him, his days of tenancy were drawing to a close. He would soon be the tenant of a very dark narrow place.

The laird stamped his foot and snorted and straightened his cravat and called for his horse.

The farmer's wife even coaxed the island children to come about the open door and jeer at the hump under the blankets. 'Slugabed! Slugabed! Slugabed!' they chanted. But when the farmer turned his melancholy eyes on them they were frightened and ran away.

In those days there were no medical men in the islands. When a person was sick, some wise old woman was sent for who knew the spells appropriate to every sickness. The wise old woman of Rousay was sent for, but she could not discover what ailed the patient. His heart-beat was steady, his forehead was cool, he ate and drank his usual, he had no pain anywhere in his body. It was something totally outside her experience. There was nowhere for her to tie her cunning knots.

'There's nothing else for it,' said the old woman, 'the trow doctor will have to be sent for. I can do nothing. It's a serious business.'

In the island of Shapinsay, a mile or two to the south of Rousay, lived a good-for-nothing young fellow. He was so lazy that it was difficult to get any work out of him at all. Oh no, he didn't think he would go to the fishing this morning. No, he wasn't in the mood to clip the ears of the sheep, not at the moment. If the folk of the district didn't mind, he would rather not cut peats with them that day ... He had a new tune, he said, that he must try out on his pipe.

The lazy creature spent most of his days wandering about in the fields with his pipe, scattering a few random notes in the wind.

It was hard to be a ploughman or a fisherman and see that idle one drifting here and there on the wind like gossamer.

After sunset he had the island to himself. Then, in the twilight, he was alone with his music. Ordinary decent country folk stay indoors at that mysterious time of the day. Occasionally, one would peer through his window and see the scalliwag on the hillside, silhouetted against the dregs of the light, with his pipe askew in his mouth, and weird music spilling out of it (not a bit like the familiar reels that they stamped and spun and skirled to in the barns). And sometimes the islanders would see, under the stars, the wastrel dancing to his own music – whirling round and round, bowing, advancing and retreating, turning on a lissom toe ... No wonder – said the Shapinsay folk – the lazy rascal was never fit for his work in the morning.

But one benighted traveller discovered the truth about the solitary music-maker. Returning home one midnight from a visit to his sweetheart who lived at the opposite end of the island, this man heard on the wind the scamp's music, a few frail notes. He decided, out of curiosity, to follow the sounds to their source. As he went on, the music became louder and clearer. The midnight wanderer crossed a little rise and saw below him, in a hill hollow, the piper sitting on a stone. He was not alone either. The dell was full of the 'peedie folk' and they were dancing and dipping round the music like moths about a still flame. There were thousands of these unearthly creatures on the hillside. If the piper paused for even a few seconds to get his breath, they pleaded with him to go on – he must – they insisted, cajoled, threatened, kissed his cunning fingers. Then once more the lazy thing would set the pipe to his mouth.

The intruder lurked for a while in the shadows beyond the music and the dance. He – like all the Orkney people of that time – knew of the 'peedie folk's' love of music. They feed with lust and passion and delight on the honey of sound. Musicians, of all men, are dear to them.

But if an ordinary inquisitive mortal like himself were to blunder into their lyrical circles, there was no knowing what terrible thing they might do to him – they might tear him to pieces, or drag him to their chambers under the hill and chain him there in the darkness for ever.

He turned. He took his wild heartbeats home with him. As he stumbled at last among the friendly croft-lights, the sweet terrible music faded away . . .

The 'peedie folk' are not ungrateful for the music that they love so dearly. They bestow gifts in exchange for rhythm and pattern – insight, it may be, or wisdom, or fore-knowledge. To the Shapinsay piper they gave a rare present – the gift of healing.

Because he was a master of cures the islanders dared not get rid of the idle creature. If the minister got toothache, for example, or the fisherman's child had a fever, he was the one they sent for. Once an old spinster in her hut at the shore began to act queerly and to mutter to herself. 'She's lost her wits,' said the island folk. The good-for-nothing visited the poor distracted one and spoke sweetly to her for an hour or so, and the next morning she was at her spinning-wheel again, as right as rain, quite resigned to being a respectable single childless old gossip for the rest of her days.

It was to this miracle-worker that the Rousay farmer's wife came one day at seed-time. She told him the strange sorrowful tale of her husband – a strong healthy man that wouldn't leave his bed because he thought he was soon going to die.

The lazy-bones nodded. He had heard of such cases before, he said. The trouble usually came about if the trows were insulted, or hurt, even though the offender might be innocent of any bad intention towards them. That was the way the 'peedie folk' took their revenge. A person couldn't be too careful.

He held out his hand. His services were not free, he implied. The magic of silver would make a difference to his diagnosis and cure. He mentioned to the Rousay woman that they didn't give free mugs of ale in the Shapinsay alehouses, especially to the likes of him. And he often got thirsty. It came from playing his pipe so much.

The farmer's wife put her last shilling into his palm. He pocketed it. Then he picked up his pipe and sketched a brief pattern of notes in the air. To the farmer's wife that little tune meant nothing, except that the fellow was more than a little crazy. But the trows, busy with their metals and springs and seed-care under the hill, knew at once what the signal meant: 'Listen, earth-creatures, little friends. That Rousay farmer – the one that broke into your chambers with his spade last summer and let a ray of hurtful light in. (I have just been composing a new reel for you.) Of course you remember him. His goodwife has given me a shilling to buy ale. (Tonight, at midnight, dear ones, this new music.) Now let the knot be loosed . . .'

To the farmer's wife he said, 'That'll be all right then.'

'Where's your herbs and your ointments?' said the farmer's wife. 'Come now. The boat's waiting. The tide's just right for Rousay.'

The lazy-bones said he wouldn't be sailing to Rousay that day. He didn't like the sea all that much. He bade her good-day.

At that the farmer's wife began to lament. 'You took my money and you won't even come and see him! You vagabond! It's true what the Shapinsay people say about you, you lazy idle good-for-nothing waster that you are!'

He told her to go home and not be stupid. If there was one thing he hated, he said, it was a nagging stupid old woman. Then he picked up his pipe once more and played a few carefree notes.

She went down to the boat in tears. Her errand had been fruitless. The boatman rowed her across. She had done everything to save her husband that mortal power could do, and the trow doctor was a cheat. There was nothing now for her man and herself and her bairns but eviction, starvation, and death.

When she came up from the shore of Rousay she saw her farm-steading, and beyond it a sower casting seed in the furrows, and singing to himself, and sometimes stopping to shake a seed-dripping fist at the rooks.

The boy and the girl ran round the house in the sun and wind, laughing.

She stood mute with joy on the road.

The curse of the 'peedie folk' had been lifted from the breadwinner at last.

George Mackay Brown
Pictures in the Cave 75p

Sigurd played truant from school one day and found himself strangely
drawn to the legendary cave where an evil witch once brewed spells
and drank the blood of children . . . Sigurd fell into conversation with
Shelmark, a seal – a magical beast, one of the mythical 'selkies'.
Shelmark unfolds the history of the cave and the island – stories that
would change Sigurd's life from that day on.

E. Nesbit
The Magician's Heart 60p

Professor Tavkin was a nice little boy when he was young but he grew
up to be an incredibly nasty person. He became a Magician – but a very
nasty one indeed. He went to royal christenings and made Prince
Fortunatus the most stupid prince in the world and Princess Aura the
most ugly princess. Many years later the stupid Prince and ugly
Princess turned the tables on him and gave him one or two nasty
shocks himself!